GENERATOR

GENERATOR

RINNY GREMAUD

Translation by Holly James

Schaffner Press
Tucson, Arizona

Copyright © 2025, Rinny Gremaud
English Translation Copyright © 2025, Holly James
Generator was originally published in French in 2023 by Sabine Wespieser Editions

First English Language Edition
Trade Paperback Original
Cover & Interior design by Hollis Duncan

Except for brief passages quoted for review, no part of this book may be reproduced in any form without the express written consent of the Publisher. Contact: Permissions Dept., Schaffner Press, PO Box 41567, Tucson, AZ 85717

Library of Congress Control Number: 2025933438

ISBN: 978-1-639640-71-3 (Paperback)
ISBN: 978-1-639640-63-8 (EPUB)
ISBN: 978-1-639640-64-5 (EPDF)

The characters and events described in this book are entirely fictitious. Any resemblances to persons living or dead are purely coincidental.

Printed in the United States

For Sook-hye and Michel
For Ulysse and Lucile
For Pierre

'For myself,' I said, 'I shall marry at once.'
Pierre Loti
Madame Chrysanthème

I was born in 1977 at a nuclear power plant in the south of South Korea.

I never thought about things that way until that day in the summer of 2017, when I read an announcement that President Moon Jae-In was planning to phase out nuclear power, starting by pulling the plug on its oldest reactor, Kori 1. My reactor.

It was the symbolic end of an era, so they said. South Korea, which had entered the nuclear age and thus a period of modernity forty years prior, was now going to invest exclusively in renewable energies. End of story, curtain, new chapter.

South Korea was not the only country to question its relationship with atomic energy back then. Nor was it the first. In 2011, Fukushima had caused a groundswell in more ways than one. And besides, forty years is the average life expectancy of a nuclear power plant—in other words, the time the owners give themselves to recoup the costs. These infrastructures, if well-maintained and regularly serviced, have the potential to last beyond this arbitrary expiration date provided the right investments are made at the right time. But the world's nuclear power plants, built primarily between the 1960s and 1980s, have been caught in a perpetual cycle of promises and setbacks, pawns in the shifting politics inherent in most industrialized democracies. At the time South Korea issued its statement, the majority of countries with nuclear facilities were faced with the decision of what to do with these gargantuan structures, as they charged en masse toward their official expiration date. The nuclear industry appeared to be having its midlife crisis.

It would be worth reflecting, I thought, on the end of this era: the first atomic age. The loss of industrial optimism, the belief in progress that once drove our societies, the power of the energy that rules our lives and governs our wealth. There is so much to say on the atomic dream, a nuclear utopia of turbine cathedrals, promises of heat and light expressed in megawatts, and the people who believed they were doing the right thing by making humanity a prisoner to comfort. So much to say, too, on the anti-nuclear faith, the new public and media consensus that went hand in hand with what had become a generalized and institutionalized mistrust of all forms of power, from science, through industry, to politics. Between 1977 and 2017, the world changed beyond recognition.

More than that, I realized that the shutdown of the Kori 1 reactor was a personal matter to me. The report from South

Korea had unearthed something in the depths of my conscience, a sediment so old I thought it had turned to stone. With the power station coming to the end of its life, the outlines began shifting around the shadows of my past, the way the aftershock of a distant earthquake quietly dislodges the lid of a tomb that's been sealed for centuries.

The announcement was timely, as I myself had just turned forty, and it resonated in a peculiar way, in a hollow tucked away somewhere in the bedrock of my identity. Perhaps the time had come for me, too, to declare the end of an era.

FORTY YEARS PRIOR, Kori 1 was officially launched. But despite having worked on this industrial feat alongside thousands of other people from a dozen different countries, my mother did not join in with the toast to celebrate the future. On the third floor of one of ten identical apartment blocks that had been hastily built and furnished in the Western style—which meant manifestly progressive, intellectually and morally—she was sitting in a rocking chair, cradling an infant just a few weeks old. Sometimes babies can be contagiously soothing, and I wonder if the weight of my tiny body asleep on her breast was enough to quell the very legitimate anxieties that must have been plaguing her at that moment in her life, momentarily drowning them in oxytocin. With Kori complete, her professional assignment was coming to an end. Was she worried about her economic future? Hardly likely. South Korea was in the midst of a period of development driven by the Cold War, and was being drip fed by the United States. It needed women like her, perfectly fluent in English, to assist the teams of Western engineers passing through the country.

Her fears must have been of a different kind. What would become of her baby when the time came for the father's scheduled departure? What would become of her, the single mother of a wide-eyed girl whose father would never acknowledge paternity? With Kori complete, the child's father, a British engineer, would leave South Korea for another continent and disappear from both of their lives.

As she rocked back and forth in the chair, the air humid in anticipation of summer's ambush, perhaps she allowed herself to succumb to reverie. What good does it do to wallow in sadness? When the future is unclear, it's better to take comfort in illusions that lighten the heart. Through the tinted glass of her own yearning, she was not the disgraced mother of an illegitimate child, but the proud embodiment of a love made impossible by convention.

As for me, I grew up not knowing why this man—a man who had loved my mother and held me in his arms, who was well aware of how vulnerable we were—had not done more to protect us.

In a time and place where a situation like ours was highly irregular, all that was to follow would require courage and tenacity. Everything was also contingent on a chance encounter with a man generous enough to open his heart, not only to my mother, but also to another man's child.

I was born forty years ago, to a resilient mother and a man I barely know a thing about, in a nuclear power plant in the south of South Korea.

I was born in Kori 1, to a proud, determined mother and a man who may well be a bastard.

I grew up on intimate terms with hypotheses, metabolizing shadows. Half of me is made of the unknown; every strand of my DNA is threaded with questions to which I've never sought answers. Silence is at the core of my being.

The word "generator" resounded throughout my childhood, echoing here and there. It's a word that fascinated me for reasons I never quite managed to put my finger on.

It seemed to mean many things at once: generator as in genitor, birth, and spark.

Generator as in father.

For forty years, the ambivalent energy generated by this absentee seemed to propel me and hold me back in equal measure. Is it dangerous to live with a reactor in the heart? Failure of cooling systems can lead to core meltdown. And I don't know if the people around me, the people I love, would ever survive the toxic radiation.

HOLYHEAD

The street where you were born is lined with rows of low, angular buildings that tail off the further you get from the town center. Elegant, three-story, Victorian constructions crowned with square turret windows above and triple-pane bow windows below, each lined with flowerbeds full of begonias and climbing roses. Along the gentle hill leading down to the sea, the houses become increasingly modest, their proportions more compact and features more dilapidated towards the outskirts. At the far end of the town, there are only around ten houses lumped together on the left, a long row of sad, gray, pebbledash facades overlooking the path, each pierced by a single sash window and a wooden door that opens onto a narrow, cramped, ground-floor interior. These are most likely redbrick houses, whose original brickwork would have been exposed until late last century.

I see you as a child, slamming one of those doors shut and hurtling down the grassy hill toward the beach on a sunny day, leaping like a cat across the black rocks spotted yellow with lichen that surround a small strip of sand below. There, safe from the tide, you leave your patchwork shirt and a pair of pants, too short for you as always, and you splash water over your growing body before launching into a freestyle on the clear, green waters of the Irish Sea.

Sometimes—perhaps, I'm making it up—you, John, and Ken dig out the fishing gear stashed away between two large rocks, equipment you cobbled together from remnants of net, bits of shrapnel, woven rushes, and wood whittled down with a pen knife: finders, keepers. You run to the water with the gear on your back, and your long strokes take you all the way out to the cut-stone breakwater, the longest of the empire, constructed by Victorian engineers as a port for Irish freighters. On the interior facade of the construction, halfway to the square lighthouse at the end, you know how to find the exact spot where irregularities in the stone provide ledges for your hands to grasp and your feet to tread. Up on the breakwater, you cast your lines and watch the steamers come in, imagining yourself as captain, as you wait for your partners in crime to arrive.

What remains in you, bitter old man, of the bitter cold sea and the rocks and the heaths that shaped the days of your childhood? Does your body remember the waves, the feeling of weightlessness, holding your breath as a game or a challenge? And the smell of charred potatoes on the fire when you set off on your expeditions, just a group of kids? Do you remember the swell of the streams in spring that revive the land and make the brambles quiver, the bleating of sheep and the barking of dogs? And the companies of gannets clinging to the rocky peaks surrounding South Stack lighthouse, its reassuring light, coming and going, the roar of the storms, the wind that fells the trees, bending bodies in two, the tremendous procession of clouds racing across a fretful sky? Do you remember, old man, all the things I see as I look for you?

IT'S WINTER. At the point on the map where Wales reaches out toward Ireland, Holyhead is braving a raging sea. From behind a dirty, plastic porthole, I see the first hazy outline of the little town appear in the crook of an indistinct mineral mass. Slowly, it solidifies into a dark cluster of waterlogged buildings caught between raging seas and a sky that's caving in, held hostage by two petulant masses of water that seem to merge into the icy gusts of wind.

He was born in this town. Eighty-two years later, what remains of him here? The ghosts of childhood, the distant branches of a family tree, a cemetery, perhaps, whose headstones might offer me clues about him. I'm more sure to find the town council, its archives, the sound of a language and rhythms of a culture, all the things a place can say for itself. The whispering of the elements, the eternal monologue of the earth, geography directly addressing the body, light that speaks to eyes and wind to skin, the smell of plants saturated with salt from the root, the terrain that quickens the heart, the distinctive bite of cold and damp combined, the density of the shade, the frequency of the waves and vibrations, unbroken throughout the ages, bringing bodies together across history, reuniting them in the intimacy of shared knowing. In this place he once knew, I'll take those sensations and make them my own, inhabit his body just for a while.

I'll arrive by boat—he was, after all, a sailor. A marine engineering mechanic, to be precise, trained on the docks of Holyhead, an industrial port that flourished with the arrival of the steam engine before free-market liberalism brought economic decline. But he didn't stay. In Holyhead or the maritime trade. His was the golden generation that postwar industry blessed with bright and varied prospects. His expertise in steam turbines meant the world was his oyster. He'd already left by the time Margaret Thatcher obliterated this town.

Perhaps you don't dream of becoming a sailor when you're pushed inexorably toward the sea by economic and geographic determinism.

Perhaps you develop romantic ideas about becoming a vicar or a banker instead. Like all young boys in this town, he would have grown up with the certainty that one way or another, be it on the docks or at sea, his future was in the merchant navy. Like the navy, only less exotic. Holyhead was the child of a fruitful relationship between Dublin and London. The need to transport mail, goods, livestock, workers, and the bourgeoisie between the capitals of the two countries made the port prosper to the point of becoming eminently strategic. Over the course of the 19th century, the

Crown invested in infrastructures here that were the only ones of their kind in the world, like the mile-and-a-half-long breakwater that took twenty-eight years to construct. Powered by steamboats and locomotives, the town became rich and cosmopolitan for at least half a century, the purveyor of prospects for the town's youth and the envy of the agricultural hinterland that had watched it grow like an anglophone cyst on Welsh soil. But the horizons it opened up to young boys seldom stretched beyond a ninety-mile radius to the west.

Holyhead-Dublin, a shuttle for all weathers. Perhaps he never dreamed of ships because his father had been one of those commuters of sea—assistant steward, according to the Register of Births, Marriages and Deaths—on one of the three boats belonging to the London Midland and Scottish Railway Company, which operated the link between Holyhead and Ireland.

Perhaps he dreamed of it all the less because, as I later learned, his father died at sea.

Holyhead: an island off an island that tapers into a teat, a rocky eminence that brings hope to the children that stand on tiptoe at its summit, trying to catch a glimpse of America.

There were three of you boys, skinny and breathless, standing there with your hands on your knees, hair in disarray, blood-rushed cheeks simmering pink and striped with dust, snot encrusted on the backs of your shirtsleeves, a coil of rope slung over one shoulder, all the gear required for the day, nails black with dirt, in need of a good scrub. Up ahead of you, exposed to the mercy of your preteen zeal, damp pathways unfurling through a mantle of short, dense, flowering vegetation, the intoxicating smell of peat and sea salt, the cries of birds. You were out looking for nests.

You had to veer off the trails and onto the thick carpet of russet leaves, occasionally perforated by the remains of a wall consumed by ivy, or a bush of one species covered in the tenacious, hardy, yellow flowers of another. With any luck, you'd find a few nests here, but more often than not, you'd have to walk along the cliff, hitch the rope onto a rock and rappel down to find the best ones, tucked away in wind-sheltered crevices between two strips of lithophytes.

You collected eggs in the same way later generations collected Pokémon cards. After church, at the weekly congregation for oologists in short pants, you would exchange your treasures and stories, because the value of the eggs was partly determined by the level of risk taken to acquire them.

You were adventurers in the effervescence of your youth, standing the test of nature, shins covered in bruises and fine hairs, ears flushed with excitement, mouths constantly chattering, making up stories about the world because you knew nothing of it, except for the odd word you'd caught from the radio set, snippets gleaned from adult conversations, the occasional etching you'd been shown in class. But that was enough for your imagination to paint landscapes that stretched for miles, populated by a host of heroic characters. In your war games there were good guys and bad guys, guns, bows and arrows, cannons, bayonets, rifles, shields and trenches. Monumental naval battles that always ended in victory for the Royal Navy. Riding elephants, you chased tigers in Madras and lions in Mombasa. You derailed trains with dynamite. You were Butch Cassidy, Lawrence of Arabia. You landed on the beaches of Normandy on your battleships. You flew Zeppelins. History was squashed beneath your dreams of glory, destinies written at the front. And in these games, you cultivated virtues: a taste for the absolute and a sense of sacrifice. You could never have imagined the century that would be yours, a century of peace, money, science and technology, mass consumption, and the selfish hedonism that goes hand-in-hand with a bloated economy. You could never have imagined all the things that would render your courage obsolete.

Of course, you had certain obligations, to the local school, the church, the community. And in certain families like yours, you had to contribute to the closed-household economy. The war had left widows in its wake. Goods remained rationed long after armistice, and you had to make do with what little you had.

But otherwise, being a boy you were allowed to disappear, sometimes for the whole day, gorging yourself on the scents of the outside world, digging, running, climbing, torturing insects, hunting amphibians, plundering nature for its intoxicating essences and treasures, discovering the infinite varieties of cold, the sun's gentle and brutal rays, the innumerable possible combinations of light and wind that taught you that there are a million skies, not just one, each one a picture in motion, movable backdrops for the vast campaigns you waged against boredom. Cutting through brambles, damming up streams, splitting through waves, clutching at rocks and conquering trees. Bending the world to your desires was a matter of physical commitment.

You didn't answer to anyone. Mothers, and still less fathers, did not constantly breathe down their children's necks as they do today. This was before the paranoid era of information overload, before the psychologization of all things, before the contraceptive pill. Before children became the prized fruits of yearning, before their decreasing numbers and the planning required to have them meant they became projects to be proud of, the way one might be proud of a new sun room; before we started raising them like potted orchids that need to be watered regularly but not too much, exposed to classical music but never direct sunlight, protected from drafts, kept indoors during the colder months. (And the moment they show signs of restlessness or appear to be withering, the moment we can no longer bear to maintain their sophisticated, vegetative lives, we hand them a cell phone, that magic window that renders legs obsolete, a window through which they can satisfy their thirst for the world by exploring the pixelated vistas of Minecraft at the tips of their fingers.)

I say *being a boy,* because for girls it was different: they had to sit at home with their legs crossed. Your sister, eight years your senior, was remarkably good at knitting. A useful skill to have in a household of modest means, because before H&M and Made in Pakistan, clothes constantly had to be repaired, sweater wool recycled, and the rest sold at the market in the form of hats and gaiters, and why not?

Your sister was beautiful. Your friends came over occasionally and would linger in the hallway in front of the kitchen door, secretly observing the mysterious contours of her adolescent body. She, engrossed in her meticulous tasks, indifferent to their presence, and they, enraptured by the eroticism of a black strand of hair slipping loose from a bun.

TALL AND DARK. That's how the people of Holyhead remember that family of unfortunates, striking as they were in their appearance. Two days after my arrival, I was left feeling shaken when an old woman pointed out the resemblance. For the first time in my life, in this unfamiliar land, in this country that does not belong to me, in this language that is not my own, she looked me in the eye and said: "I can see him in you."

ONE EVENING, there in front of the war memorial, on a plaque dedicated to the victims of 1939–1945, I spot his surname. On my glasses, rain, on my frozen hands, rain, on the screen of my phone, rain, distorting all the pixels. With both my thumbs on that square of blue light, I find an online registry dedicated to the memory of the fallen, and in less than ten minutes, hands contorted by the cold, I learn from the internet that his father died at Dunkirk.

In the still-raw air of an early May morning, I imagine the three of you taking a brisk walk toward the port, your long shadows in tow. It's five o'clock in the morning and already the horizon has all but lost its coral tinge. Above the sea, a few amber tufts wait peacefully to be washed white by the coming day.

This dream scene I painted with only my imagination for oils, on the canvas of what little information I have, depicts you with your family for the last time, on the morning your father was leaving to serve his country.

Along with most of England's large public buildings, the passenger ferry he worked on had been requisitioned for the evacuation of soldiers serving in the British Expeditionary Force. Across the channel, the troops had been defeated. The Allies had been ill-prepared and lost in the Blitz. The British retreated to Dunkirk. No more men would be sent to the front. Orders were to get out.

The *TSS Scotia* set sail for Southampton, where it would be waiting within two hours to leave for Dover. William Henry Hughes' crew of thirty-seven men was proud to contribute to the war effort. The assistant steward, who had only ever sailed one route, would finally get to go further afield. They'd be calling at Pembroke, perhaps, Penzance, almost certainly, then Plymouth, Exmouth, Weymouth, and Bournemouth, before arriving in Southampton on May 26.

The men did not know when they would return. The atmosphere on the docks was electric. The children had come to wave them off, the women were dressed in their Sunday best. In a plume of black smoke, the ship's two funnels began to slip away from the port. On paper, this was no different from any other day, except hearts weren't beating in the same way.

A few weeks after the disaster, your mother learns from a letter, say, that her husband is never coming back. She breaks down in tears.

Or maybe a young man in uniform turns up at the door to deliver the news. Maybe she holds back her tears and goes back into the kitchen with a look of indifference on her face. Feigned or genuine? It's impossible to tell.

Or maybe no letter ever arrives. At church or at the market, Captain Hughes' wife delivers the news that the *Scotia* has sunk at Dunkirk. There were casualties, yes, but aside from the captain, who is known to be safe and sound, nobody knows what became of the men. The surviving crew members are to be brought to Holyhead by train. But the day the train pulls into the station, your father is not among them. An employee of London Midland Scottish Railway is sent to put up a list of the dead, and it's there, in your mother's distraught expression, in the midst of this gathering, where intense joy rubs shoulders with intense pain, in the silent anguish breaking like a wave through the tight crowd, that you understand, at the tender age of five, that your father is never coming back. His death, a complete abstraction, is the invisible center of gravity amongst all the commotion, the source of your mother's tears, the presence embedded in the frozen panic sweeping over her.

What grounds do I have for allowing myself to switch from the cautious conditional of inquiry to the self-assured affirmative of fiction, with no other claim than the universal right to daydream?

One day, during a visit to Holyhead's little maritime museum—an old hangar whose adjoining spaces are overflowing with unlikely treasures, maps, plans, models, and relics collected by generations of enthusiasts—I happen upon the president of the association that keeps the museum alive. Tourists are few and far between in November, so it doesn't take long for someone to ask me what I'm doing here. I'm following the footsteps of a man, I say, and I tell him your name.

When I say it, my interlocutor's face lights up, and he tells me with a broad smile that the man I'm looking for was one of his childhood friends. There were three of them: Jim,

Ken, and John, always out on the moor, ransacking birds' nests and making fires to cook potatoes.

We arrange to meet the following day. He'll drive me to the places they used to go as children, summoning memories that, at his age, are clearer in his mind than the things that happened just yesterday. He'll introduce me to his cousin, who in turn knows someone who knows someone else who remembers the man I'm looking for. That someone will then dig out an old notebook from the bottom of a drawer, containing the following crucial piece of information: a mail address in Michigan. An address from almost thirty years ago, but an address, nonetheless.

Modern technology works its magic, online directories cross-reference old addresses with new ones on interactive maps. I thought I was following the tracks of a dead man. But the object of my investigation turns out to be very much alive, the owner of a house visible on satellite images.

I decide to write him. No reply.

WHAT IF I made you into a fiction? I could make a ghost of you, condemn you to the shadows, forever trapped in the web of my imagination.

Just as constellations are drawn by tracing imaginary lines, I'll constitute a genitor for myself from the little information I have: your apprenticeship as a mechanical engineer at the Port of Holyhead, those years of service at Trinity House, the UK lighthouse authority, a marriage in Taiwan, where your first two children were born, a stint in South Korea for the now defunct GEC Turbine Generators, where you met my mother, your departure for Monroe in the United States, the birth of two more children with the same mother as the first, and finally, your last known address in Michigan.

With these milestones as a guide, the rest is mine. I'll do a little digging, I'll find the power plants on your curriculum vitae, some nuclear, some thermal, equipped with turbines made by GEC and English Electric, a company that was eventually absorbed by the former, both of which must have employed you at some stage. I'll match the commissioning dates with the births of your children. I'll travel the landscapes you've known and paint a backdrop for you. I'll take my investigation to the places and industries that were once yours. And, since I have no choice, I'll mix the facts with the water of my imagination, knead you a life as if out of clay.

It doesn't matter whether you find this life resembles your own, it doesn't matter if you protest. If you didn't want it to be this way, all you had to do was tell me the story yourself. All you had to do was reply to my letter. It was your cowardice that gave me my omnipotence.

You come hurtling down the narrow staircase, your tender face framed by a brilliantine wave. Outside, the half-light of the early morning and the fog endemic to the season make a bleary silhouette of your neighborhood. Your mother is waiting for you in the small, dimly lit living room, on her feet as always, mechanically dusting an ornament on the mantelpiece. You've never seen her sitting on the patterned velvet armchairs cluttering up the room, their backs and arms covered with white doilies to keep them clean. When she's not at the stove, she's knitting or crocheting on a wooden chair beneath a bare lightbulb at the foot of the stairs, halfway between the hallway and the kitchen.

In the cramped confines of this post-war living room, it seems as though she's half your size, obscured by your adolescent frame. The clothes handed down to you by your father and brother are all too short in the sleeves.

Your mother has grown pale over the last ten years, the thin, wrinkled skin around her wrists and eyes becoming translucent. It's been a long time since a smile spread across her cheeks, which delicately droop around her mouth.

She comes up to you, fixes the collar of your blue shirt, inspects your clean-shaven face, running the backs of her fingers along your jawline. Then she takes a step back, plunges one of her dry, bony hands into the pocket of her apron, pulls out a pack of cigarettes and a box of matches and places them in your hands like the most precious of treasures. Finally, her eyes riveted to yours, she makes an awkward but solemn declaration: "You're a man now." Then she embraces you and adds in a whisper: "Don't say a word to your brother."

Turning away to hold back the tears, she busies herself again before returning with a bundle of things—your sandwich box, your flask, and your iron cup—as you put on your flat cap and slip a worn-out peacoat on top of your overalls. Outside, the shadows preceding the dawn seem to be creeping in through the door. From the street, you turn and wave affectionately, before your lanky legs carry you to the top of the road where you disappear. It's an extravagant gift your mother has given you; cigarettes are a luxury for a welfare family like yours.

Ten years after your father's death, your sister has become a mother herself. Your brother, an industrial foreman twelve years your senior, has left Holyhead for Liverpool and taken a well-paid job to support you and your mother. These, of course, are all figments of my imagination. No matter… who is there to contradict me?

One morning in January 1951, you, too, become an adult. The first light marks your sixteenth birthday and the first day of your apprenticeship. These will be your golden years, as the cliché goes. What man doesn't have vivid memories of his youth? Besides, an apprenticeship on the dockyard is a privilege. Ships of all shapes and sizes dock in Holyhead, sometimes from far-flung places. Soon, you'll come to know by heart the names of the entire merchant fleet sailing England's North West Coast: who charters, who commands, who carries what, to where and for whom, what kind of motor, what output, tonnage, speed. Each vessel is a unique feat of mechanical engineering, the cumulative pride of dozens of teams, hundreds of men, who, year after year, generation after generation, have taken turns to build and assemble its components and navigate the whole ingenious assembly, loading, unloading, steering, securing, docking, alerting, maintaining, repairing and loving, yes, loving those ships, the vessels they had created that would long outlive them. Is that not why men speak of having served on a ship, and never of the ship having served them?

The shipyard brings together all types of trades: timber, iron, electricity. Apprentice engineers like you, the cream of the crop, are known as the "brainy" ones. Days are long at technical school. Here, you'll learn about corporatism, social class, and social life—that is, life in the company of men— in the everyday violence of the post-war period.

As part of the habitual bullying and hazing that no one escapes, they send you one day to a hangar on some plausible pretext or other. Suddenly, you find yourself the center of a jeering mob. They take off your pants and underpants and paint your genitals with tar. "Count yourself lucky," your strapping tormentors jibe, because others before you have found themselves in a similar state only out at sea, hanging by their jackets from the ship's crane, bare-assed on the water, the viscous liquid drying between their legs.

As a mechanical engineer, you learn the names and functions of all the parts of a steam engine: cylinders, pistons, crossheads, crankshafts, connecting rods and rod heads—the detailed anatomy of a mechanics for the subjugation of fluids. And behind all these words, the volumes and weights, the movements and intricacies, the materials, whether cold, greasy, combustible, motile, conductive, fragile, heavy, obsolescent, odorous (or is that just the oil?), every part has its unique properties, its noises and needs. From what first seems like a cacophony of indiscernible sounds, your ear learns to pick out the song of each element in motion and the signals that are cause for alarm. Certain components, for example, give off a nutty smell when overheated, while others begin to rattle like a waltz in triple time.

You discover the magical power of fire, which has the ability to draw from water an expansive force, one capable of moving matter, setting the world in motion. At school you put numbers and letters to this phenomenon, the laws of physics, which at first seem to be nothing but rigid formulas, but which you soon come to understand as the rules to a game of possibilities, an art that makes the elements bend to man's will.

In the waiting room to employment, a place of duty without any privilege, you observe the harmonious coexistence of formal and informal hierarchies, a thousand and one petty ways of getting around regulations. You learn that courage comes at a higher cost than dishonorable behavior. You experience the intoxicating joys of being part of a collective, moving in time with the rhythm of a team. You meet brothers and fathers. You feel a sense of belonging.

When you leave the shipyard, you follow the rest of your team to the pub. But the pittance you're paid each month doesn't get you very far. If you want to drink, smoke, or be in with the chance of touching a woman's breasts, you have to rely on your colleagues' generosity.

Increasingly, your mother finds herself sitting at home alone in the evening. During these formative years, you experience for the first time a new kind of exhaustion; not the wild, liberating release of energy from the body you felt as a child, nor the happy exhaustion that comes with playing ball games or chase, but a dull restless fatigue building up in the spine that comes as a result of constant obedience. A weariness that cannot be cured by sleep but can be anesthetized by alcohol.

In this portrait of you from sixteen to twenty, I imagine the habits and pastimes of a place, time, and social class that black and white television was yet to reach. Books were a rarity, to be read time and again. Walks through open fields, singing with friends. On Sundays, you would still take your mother's arm at church.

But who were you really at that age? A fervent age, as novels would have it, Fauvist, if it were a painting, intense and full of contrast, smells, and sensuality. An age when it feels like everything is brimming over and everything hurts, when the body's tissues are inflamed with desire for tomorrow, for eternity. Who were you when the West was rewriting and reconstructing itself, planting its optimistic ideals like crocuses? Which side were you on, which party did you belong to? Where was your heart in the springtime of all things?

AT THE MARINA café in Holyhead, on a day when the wind was whistling through the shrouds in a forest of masts, one of your classmates (who had the honor, at the end of his career, of serving as head mechanic on the legendary *Queen Elizabeth II*) was stirring up memories over a steaming cup of bergamot tea.

From these haphazard remembrances emerges a portrait of a young man who, at every opportunity, would impress anyone listening by reciting endless poems or theatrical monologues, rhythmical sequences of words he would effortlessly reel off, by heart and without any mistakes.

This distinctive plasticity of memory, the ability to retain and reproduce rhythms, sounds, tones and accents is one I know well. When I was younger, I was the same.

Today, I see it clearly in my children.

WYLFA

ONE MINUTE YOU'RE twenty years old, and the next, you've turned thirty. Here you emerge, fully formed, a blue-collar worker earning a living, emancipated from your family apart from your mother's upkeep. With the Empire disintegrating, the Cold War setting in, and the machine industry flourishing, capitalism and science are greater allies than ever before. There's the women you love, the ships whose engines you've been entrusted with. But there's no need to go into these events in any greater length or depth than this handful of words, because, let's face it: haven't we lingered in Holyhead a little too long?

You cut your teeth in the poverty of the post-war years, this much we must remember, in your defense and in the defense of your generation (against what accusation, exactly?).

Duly certified as a marine engineering mechanic, you set sail along the coasts of England and Wales, the Channel

Islands and Gibraltar, wherever lighthouses and lifebuoys fall by royal decree under the responsibility of Trinity House, the noble corporation that employs you for ten years.

Trinity House: the UK's lighthouse authority. Its name alone is the stuff of dreams. But time is short and an international career awaits you. I'll just mention one detail that came up in my investigation (your classmate remembered one day and told me in the last letter he sent to me before his death): you served for a time in Penzance on the *THV Stella,* the third diesel-electric lighthouse tender belonging to the "Mermaid" class (THV being Trinity House Vessel). On this ship, you traveled the length of the Cornish peninsula, eastwards as far as Start Point, and north-eastwards as far as Trevose Head, witnessing each day with increasing indifference—for the capacity to marvel dwindles with time—a procession of phenomenal landscapes: sheer cliffs bathing in clear, foamy water, grassy, undulating, wild moors tousled by the wind.

I could have written a book on the white majesty of the buildings you visited, buildings you helped refuel and maintain, their Cyclops-like dignity, the hackneyed sentiments they inspire. Lighthouses poised in their reclusive solitude, a symbol of permanence in the face of the elements, the feats and determination to which they owe their existence. No doubt I would have written a fine book on those lighthouses if, in the mid-sixties, you hadn't changed course for a career in the nuclear industry.

From 1965 onwards in Wylfa, on the Isle of Anglesey, the nuclear construction site of the century begins recruiting qualified engineers. And you, you know all there is to know about the power of steam and how it makes pistons dance, the latest developments in the science of thermodynamics. Professionally speaking, you've reached full maturity and power. You have practical experience, ambitions no doubt, and, as we would say today, several years' experience in team and project management. You've proven yourself to be flexible, employable, responsible, and compliant. And perhaps that's why, after a decade in Cornwall, you feel as though the Wylfa nuclear power plant is calling you back into the fold. It's a good opportunity and you grab it with both hands: the chance to change course for a life filled with megatechnologies and maxiturbines.

On the precipice of a wild, rocky coastline, the power station towers like castles once did over a Welsh landscape battered by the sea. All around, farmlands glittering with streams and bestrewn with cattle languishing beneath a low sky. So picturesque, it could be the subject of a painting by William Turner. As far as I can ascertain (and particularly outside of France), nuclear power plants tend to occupy sumptuous landscapes, perhaps insofar as their requirements converge to an extent with those of the fanciful tourist: they like to be a good distance from populous metropolitan areas and they seek a base of solid rock where they can bathe their circuits in cool sea water.

The Kori power station in South Korea occupies a stretch of coastline that is—or at least once was—curiously similar to the coast of Wylfa, with its rich polyphony of greens frayed with squat, anthracite cliffs and dotted with short, sandy beaches. But that was before South Korea's demographic growth brought cranes and cement mixers and deformed the phenomenal natural landscape, a fate it did not share with Anglesey.

While two different sites were still under consideration as potential locations for the future nuclear power plant in Wales, there was just one old woman living in an isolated cottage who voiced her unequivocal opposition to such a contraption being built on her doorstep. Without further elaborating, she declared: "Over my dead body," (which in Welsh would have been something to the effect of *dros fy nghrogi* according to an online dictionary).

This anecdote appears in an unlikely cultural anthropology thesis written in the 1980s by a student at the University of Nijmegen in the Netherlands on the decline of Welsh as a spoken language in the village of Camaes near Wylfa. It was only when I read this study that it occurred to me for the first time that the man who brought me into this world might have spoken this language.

A quick internet search revealed that seventy-four percent of school-age children living in Holyhead in 1951 spoke Welsh, and, to be completely honest, it made me a little sad to find myself here, putting these questions to American algorithms, when there's nothing more intimate, more significant than the sounds of the words we give to things, the grammar that structures the way we see. There is nothing more distinctive than the intrinsic rhythm of the language or languages we speak.

We don't have the same idea of a man who speaks Italian, for example, as we would if we knew he also spoke Friulian.

We paint a different portrait of a French person if we neglect to mention the fact she also speaks Basque. And the fact that I've been reduced to forming hypotheses based on search engine results about whether the man who brought me into the world was a Welsh speaker, whether out of family loyalty, predilection, or even vanity… it makes me angry. Because deep down, if I stopped lying to myself for a moment, I'd admit that I'd rather be asking him these questions.

Back in Anglesey, or *Ynys Môn* in Welsh, a different site was eventually chosen for the plant, on the doorstep of another cottage no doubt, and at that time, at the turn of the 1960s, not a single person in the whole of North Wales protested against the installation of those two nuclear reactors, which would be the largest, most powerful of their kind in the world. On the contrary, the initiative was applauded by inhabitants and local authorities alike, as it would mean sustainable employment and long-term prosperity.

Apparently no one dared to ask questions at the information meeting organized by the investment consortium (British Nuclear Design and Constructions) for fear that the small fishing and farming community would miss out on the economic windfall it so badly needed.

Eventually, one man plucked up the courage to ask: "What will you do with the waste?" A besuited official immediately responded: "We're very close to finding a solution. Don't worry about that aspect of the technology. Everything is under control."

The Swinging Sixties, a time of industrial optimism.

AFTER THE SECOND WORLD WAR ended, Great Britain was preparing itself psychologically and materially to single-handedly fight an enemy that was yet to be named. Britain's "special relationship" with the United States, which had led to the two countries merging their nuclear programs, was steadily disintegrating, and the Crown set about building its own nuclear reactors to produce weapons of mass destruction.

That was when the Ministry of Defense came up with an idea: why not kill two birds with one stone and recycle the immense quantity of heat emitted by the manufacture of plutonium by transforming it into electricity? That was in 1955.

Plutonium was proclaimed to be the new gold by economists working for the military. Thanks to its value, which would only increase over the coming years, the electricity it generated would cost next to nothing, and all the capitalists in the country would be queuing up to purchase permission to construct nuclear power stations. Science, technology, and the free market would bring the nation greatness, if its economists were to be believed.

Duly convinced, the country's honorable MPs signed up to an unprecedented ten-year plan that very year: 300 million pounds of taxpayers' money would be invested in the construction of twenty-six magnox nuclear reactors across eleven power plants, financed through private investment consortia. These plants would have the dual function of cooking up the stuffing for Her Majesty's thermonuclear warheads, while simultaneously lighting up the homes of her loyal subjects. Wylfa was to be the last site in this vast program.

Magnox (short for magnesium non-oxidizing) is a magnesium-aluminum alloy used for cladding nuclear fuel in large tubes—in this case, tall, round pellets of natural uranium that look like Rolos, only black. Each of these tubes was the size of a roll of wrapping paper, except they weighed around forty pounds apiece. The Wylfa power plant contained just under fifty thousand of these stubby elements known as fuel rods. The rods were inserted into the reactor in sets of eight and would be removed periodically from one of the plant's upper floors above the reactor vessel, a process involving a great deal of patience and difficulty, according to records. The reactor vessel was a vast structure with holes in its floor, each with its own coordinates, leading directly to the reactor core. Naturally, this design raised a few questions about ionizing radiation, but in those days, a reactor vessel with holes in it was considered preferable to none at all (bearing in mind this was also a time before cars were fitted with seatbelts). Unlike in today's power plants, fuel was loaded and unloaded while the reactor was active, using a large machine resembling a lighthouse on wheels driven by a guy in a white coat—perhaps a freshly graduated nuclear physics student being hazed.

To understand this peculiar phenomenon, or what now seems peculiar in light of how the industry has evolved and modern society's collective intolerance to risk, we first need to go through a few technical explanations that will take us all the way inside this reactor, to the infinitesimally small particles that make up those little black pellets.

According to the computer-generated animations available on the internet, the chain reaction at the heart of a nuclear power plant's operations is simply a matter of little green, blue and red balls bouncing off one another in slow motion, in the directions indicated by the arrows onscreen. In reality, it's a chaotic but calculable projection of microscopically small particles, which can rocket up to more than twelve thousand miles per second and, with any luck, crash into other atomic nuclei. The fission of these nuclei will emit new, similarly fast particles, which in turn will break other nuclei, and so on—all the while releasing very large quantities of heat. The whole art of nuclear power, the whole science behind its industrialization, lies in the ability to moderate this powerful phenomenon, i.e. to use materials that are neither too fissile nor insufficiently so, to ensure that the right number of neutrons breaks the right number of nuclei without the machine ever overheating.

In order to achieve this, these ultra-fast neutrons must be paired with a material inside the reactor that slows them down. In early civil nuclear programs, the favored material was graphite. The heat, meanwhile, is regulated through the circulation of a liquid or gas fluid, which is then harnessed in the form of steam. In short, a nuclear power station is essentially a sophisticated kettle that generates steam to drive its turbines.

Magnox reactors had a graphite core filled with natural uranium and were cooled using carbon dioxide. The funny thing is that uranium in this particular state is primarily made up of material unsuitable for energy production. Or, as the specialists would have it: 99.3% of it is made up of a non-fissile isotope (U238). Non-fissile means that even when bombarded with neutrons, the nucleus will not break.

Why, then, did the British go to such lengths, to the point of constructing twelve power plants, to take enormous quantities of a material unsuitable for producing energy and bombard them with neutrons? Because, as we have seen, they were trying to kill two birds with one stone. U238 tends to absorb neutrons it comes into contact with. U238 + one neutron = Pu239 (the reality is a little more complicated but the details are of little importance here). And Pu239 is plutonium, the most effective element for making bombs with. But there is a delicate balance to this alchemy. One neutron too many, and you can end up with a mixture of Pu239 and Pu240 on your hands: an isotope that is far too fissile (unstable, in other words). And while military engineering requires toxic and lethal materials, it's still best if you can keep them under control. So magnox fuel rods could not remain in their eponymous reactors for too long, if the "right" plutonium was to be extracted. Hence the sieve-like reactor vessels, which made it possible to load and unload the rods in good time without ever stopping the machine.

In the end, the Cold War lost its momentum (it's as though they did it on purpose, to prove the economists at the British Ministry of Defense wrong). The first treaty on the non-proliferation of nuclear weapons was signed while Wylfa was still under construction, and Great Britain found itself extracting energy from twenty-six reactors that had not been designed primarily for this purpose, and with more plutonium on its hands than it knew what to do with.

Magnox reactors, which are now all in the process of being dismantled, have remained a specialty almost exclusive to Britain. After plans for the plant were made public as part of a UN-led nuclear disarmament effort, only North Korea saw fit to belatedly reproduce the technology for its much-maligned nuclear program.

Back at the Wylfa plant, which would be under construction for a total of eight years, little did they know the facility would soon be obsolete. It was an astounding feat of technical and human ingenuity, up there with the likes of the Great Pyramid of Giza, Saint Peter's Basilica, the Suez Canal, the Grande Dixence Dam, and the Millau Viaduct. In terms of its size and precision, Wylfa was completely unprecedented.

At the crack of dawn, double-decker buses with their square snouts and rounded edges would arrive carrying the workers not living on site. At the same time, on-site workers came pouring from their digs like ants, and managers pulled up in front of the offices in their Ford Anglias and Austin 1100s. At the height of construction, up to two thousand six hundred men were working at the Wylfa plant every day.

Upon hectares of mud and dust, the most powerful machines of their time stormed the heavens, creating a sculpture of rolling bridges and cranes looming over two formidable reactor vessels, surrounded by a tangle of girders.

You could walk for miles before realizing you'd made barely any headway, for the size of the construction was completely disproportionate to human walking distance. From afar, it was sometimes possible to make out the movements of a tiny body, moving along like an insect on a branch. Up there, some sixty feet high, the wind blew sea water into the faces of these worker-cum-acrobats, who had neither harnesses nor protection. Hours were long, stomachs often empty, and death a very real possibility, yet these inclement conditions were a source of pride for the men. "This is no place for sissies," they can be heard saying blithely in a 1967 documentary that follows the construction of this "Nuclear Cathedral" (the title of the film).

The two reactors in Wylfa were the most monumental structures to have been produced in the history of nuclear engineering. To get an idea of their scale, imagine a cylindrical graphite mega-assembly that just about fits inside the dome of the Pantheon in Rome, complete with various elements of the primary circuit attached to it, including a heat exchanger, fans, a steam generator, and a whole array of pipes, all encased in a four-meter-thick concrete casing. And that, of course, is just one of the two reactors. A second Pantheon would therefore be required, with a space equivalent to the size of one reactor separating the two, and the whole assembly would be covered with a superstructure of windowless sheet-metal, more or less double the height of the reactors.

The apotheosis of the UK's first civil nuclear power program and the ultimate display of its industrial prowess was built to generate 980 megawatts from a technically suboptimal piece of apparatus.

The coalition of physicists and engineers had staked everything on size.

Wylfa, if you think about it, had this in common with the dinosaurs: At the dawn of a new era of microtechnology and miniaturization, it was the last specimen of a species with such excessive proportions. It was completely out of step with the world around it.

The turbine hall adjoining the reactor building was 1,300 feet long. Inside, miles of piping of all diameters, valves, shafts, wheels and blades, faucets, actuators, and bolts the size of fists, platforms and balconies surrounded by double railings, all of which were intertwined to form a landscape reminiscent of the bowels of an aircraft carrier. At the heart of this colossal steam engine, the smell of grease, iron, and paint.

There was no room for approximation here. Each worker was the guardian of a cog in the machine, responsible for flow, circulation, rotation or speed. There were men everywhere, minuscule, lying in all sorts of improbable positions like mechanics under the chassis of a car, except that here they were inside the engine itself, and sometimes even inside a cog.

The size of each component was so great that nothing could be factory-assembled. Instead, individual parts as large as overland transport would allow were delivered to the construction site to be assembled there. The beast then had to be reconstituted according to diagrams, which we might imagine drawn on gigantic rolls of parchment like the plans of a demiurge.

At this stage in your career, you are one of these silhouettes in work overalls. Not those at the very bottom, tightening and oiling the nuts and bolts, but one of the men who are required to think a little, perhaps even take initiative now and then. You were part of the intermediate tier of the hierarchy in the days before flat organizational structures became the trend.

Faced with the prospect of a life on dry land after ten years at sea, it's not unlikely you bought yourself a motorbike: a BSA, maybe even the A65 Star, seeing as you could afford it.

As you rode along on this beautiful machine you'd see the patchwork of lush pastures and stone hamlets vanish out the corner of your eye in a blur of color. The deep gurgle of the engine reverberating off the asphalt and bouncing up into the sky went straight to your head; the graceful power of your body united with the machine produced an intoxicating, giddy sensation at every bend.

Each day, just before the sun was snuffed out by the sea, you carved your way through the Welsh heaths dotted with gorse, and in springtime, carpets of mauve flowers. If the light was good, you would stop and walk to one of the spots where the moor breaks into a cascade of black rock and the pervasive winds draw a delicate line of foam along the shores of the Irish Sea. Perhaps the hares or some variety of weasel heard you reciting the verses that flowed from your lips in a long, low singsong, until at last, having reached the edge of the coast, inebriated by the open air and the solitude of your surroundings, you began to deliver lines from time immemorial at the top of your lungs, carried away in a eurythmic trance inspired by the haunting song of the untamed waters.

A few years earlier, your mother had passed away, and you no doubt returned from Penzance to clear out the house and help with the funeral. Your brother and sister had decided on the essentials. They argued over one or two objects of little value: an ornament, a book, the few photographs that remained. Your older brother had taken the box of family records with him, and the clothes—which had never been in fashion—were given to charity shops.

You learned of her death from a telegram sent by your brother. The landlady of your lodgings in Penzance watched you fold up the paper and put it in your pocket as if it had been a mere formality. Your heart was now firmly walled up behind the pragmatism of your thirties and your first thought had been of the inconvenience your absence would cause your employer.

With no family left in Holyhead, you'd been staying at the George Hotel on Market Street for the duration of Wylfa's construction. You ate at the pub each evening. Since leaving your mother, you'd never lived anywhere else, never learned to cook, that's just the way it was back then.

The waitresses liked to chat with you and would occasionally come back to your room when their shifts were over. Sometimes you'd eat with colleagues who were in the same boat. There were occasions, though much less frequent, when you were invited to dinner by someone living in Holyhead with their family in a cramped two-story house like the one you grew up in.

It was when you arrived at one of these dinners, bouquet of flowers in hand, that you met a woman. She was fairly pretty, the younger sister of your colleague's wife, and she seemed eager to start a family with whoever would take her. She had a fringe (how modern!), she wore her dresses above the knee, she lived with her mother, to whom she was very close, she could sing in tune, and she took good care of her hands. After housekeeping school, she found a job as a secretary for the council, where a vicious accounts assistant would constantly pinch her on the backside, which made her want to become a stay-at-home mother all the more. You courted her long enough to take her virginity, and together you'd walk across the heathland you knew like the back of your hand. Often you'd take her to South Stack to kiss her as the sun was setting.

One day, you arranged to meet on a bench by the sea, and you told her the news: You'd been offered a senior position, an assignment in Taiwan, a fantastic opportunity for you to advance your career. You'd be gone for two years. You'd come back.

Taiwan. It might as well have been Sumatra, Ceylon, or Bora Bora. The words didn't conjure any mental image behind the light, anxious eyes of the girl with the fringe. After making love, which was no more than a routine event by now, you parted ways with silent promises and a vow in your eyes which, once you landed in Asia, you no longer felt particularly bound by after all.

LINKOU

WHAT DID I come to Taipei for? There's nothing left of you here now. The wife you met in this city is still living by your side, according to the US Land Records website. The bonds of your marriage were practically unscathed by the love of another woman and the birth of another child in another country. Really, we were nothing more than a passing fancy.

I came to Taipei to wander the streets, to inhale the smells in the air, to scour the thick humidity with my eyes and try to make out the tops of the skyscrapers. I came to revel in the rainy season, and to walk my hypotheses through the ancient, narrow, meandering streets where potted plants overflow from low buildings with barred windows and flat roofs. I came to slurp noodle soup at the night market, to scan the Asian faces with inquisitive eyes, searching for an epiphany, searching for a woman, just as I imagine you did almost half a century ago.

Here is where you first experienced foreignness, that intoxicating feeling of complete deracination known as exoticism. Here is where I'll reconstruct your Western, male gaze on an Asia I never knew: underdeveloped as they used to say back then, newly freed from the yoke of the Japanese, assisted and instrumentalized by the victors of the Second World War, prey to the great global redistribution of powers. I'll search for traces of a time when flights from Europe to Asia cost $6,000 and had to bypass the Soviet Union. A time before automatic washing machines and cable TV, before the whole world had been converted to taking their coffee with frothy cow's milk, before salmon and avocado bagels and monogrammed handbags were considered universal essentials of a life fulfilled.

In early 1971, not long after Wylfa was first connected to the electricity grid, you left Great Britain, tasked by your employer with bringing to this region of the Far East the latest product of industrial engineering: a steam turbine for a new thermal power station.

THERE WAS A time when Taipei would rumble with the sound of mopeds, more frequent in number than cars. The buses would splutter out black smoke that settled on the city in the form of dust, blackening the facades of its squat buildings lit up with advertisement signs in Chinese. You didn't have to travel far before the city surrendered to shadows, the streetlights becoming scarcer as the hypercenter disappeared into the distance. Silence was still conceivable, broken only by the occasional crackling of a radio, the blaring of a jukebox. The vinyl stereo had only just been invented and television screens were still a rarity to be switched on only sparingly.

But the Great Acceleration was underway. The country's factories were already producing cheap electronics that would change the world. The semi-conductor industry was on the verge of turning modern society on its head. But this would require energy. A lot of energy. Linkou was one of the very first thermal power plants built in Taiwan. From the turn of the 1950s up to the 1973 energy crisis, the country's electricity was generated by burning fuel oil. To keep pace with the rapid upswing in the Taiwanese economy (that is, to keep the factories running and power the electronic devices coming out of them), two new energy production units were ordered in the mid-sixties: the first from Westinghouse in America, the second from English Electric. The provenance of this equipment was a strategic matter, a clear indication of which side of the Cold War Chiang Kai-shek was on, as well as which powers were backing the White Terror then reigning over the island. During those years, the same people were busy consolidating the power of the military junta in South Korea, building thermal then nuclear power plants there too, betting (correctly) on the principle that megaturbine-fueled capitalism would be the best bulwark against the threat of communism.

You'd set off from London on a long-haul flight with the British Overseas Airways Corporation, destined for Hong Kong. There, you took a second flight with Hong Kong Airways to Taipei and landed at the former Japanese military airport of Songshan.

The moment the aircraft door was opened, the hot, humid air rushed into the cabin. You walked down the steps, squinting in the light, your clothes instantly sticking to your skin. All around you, dreamlike beneath the waves of heat, was a kind of vegetation that you had only ever seen planted in your imagination by Kipling (or was it Conrad, or Graham Greene? What kinds of books did you read?). Everywhere, tanned faces with fine pores, plump cheeks and jet-black eyes framed with thick, black hair. To you they were the faces of eternal youth. Was it there, in the rumbling air on the tarmac, that you fell in love with Asia?

At thirty-six, you were still relatively young, probably a little disheveled. Perhaps you had a beard. Your height and the camera on a strap around your neck made you stick out at the local markets you visited dressed in a short-sleeved shirt teamed with brown, pleated, polyester pants cut high above the ankle.

In the little village of Linkou, the few Westerners you crossed paths with were USAF troops who'd been posted at the small military base US intelligence forces were using to spy on communist China from across the ocean. In Taipei, it was the soldiers who had come on R&R in the hopes of rest, or failing that, a bit of distraction from the ongoing war in Vietnam.

You weren't the same age as them, you didn't have the same haircut, and you certainly didn't have the same physique. You might have been taken for a foreign correspondent of an English-speaking media outlet. You might also have passed for a salesman selling semi-manufactured or machine tool products. What other reason would anyone have for being white in Taiwan back then? Clearly you weren't in finance, you didn't have the right look. And consultants hadn't been invented yet.

With the energy crisis on the horizon, in this global economy that seemed destined to keep growing forever, you were part of the class of workers who the world has since forgotten were at the forefront of globalization: senior executives in the secondary industry, those who wore work overalls over a white shirt and tie. Men who only ever seem to have been photographed in groups, posing shoulder to shoulder in vast hangars. Missionaries of new technologies with white helmets on their heads or under their arms, heralds of progress. Men who were paid a lot of money to create a new future: one of atomic power, supersonic aircraft, and the conquest of space. In the twenty-first century, is there anyone who still remembers that the future once belonged, not to investment bankers, reality TV heroes or professional footballers, but to the engineers of the machine industry?

In Taiwan, bathed in the aura of whiteness, you were noticed and courted. Your lofty stature and economic status suddenly made you desirable in a way you never had been in your homeland. Here, men would try to win your trust and women catch your attention. This position of dominance in the public sphere would come as a shock at first (in Britain, you were nothing, the son of a nobody) but soon enough, it would become normal to you. Soon enough, you would even delight in your new role and the eye-catching costume that came with it, one sewn together with racism and preconceptions, a costume that was once worn by colonialists and continues to be worn, albeit in a more modern iteration, by expatriates on their economic missions.

SOME TWENTY MILES to the east of the capital lies a lush little valley strewn with flat houses, cemeteries, and golf courses. Its hillsides are criss-crossed with extra-high-voltage power lines supported by majestic red-and-white pylons. The mountain unfolds, bend by bend, until eventually opening up onto a vast, sandy coastline dotted with wind turbines. A murky, beige sea laps peacefully at their feet, glistening in the sun.

There's a semblance of a village, a 7-Eleven, a bubble tea shop, a few traditional houses (some in ruins and others that have been aging in neglect since the 1960s), all clustered around the foot of the spectacular, sky-splitting chimney of Linkou Power Plant. There's a deserted playground at the edge of a parking lot. A multi-colored temple, decorated with dragons and Chinese divinities in armor, stands right beside a modern-looking visitor's center made entirely of glass behind a second, larger parking lot. Air-conditioned buses equipped with toilets bring in workers from Taipei on a daily basis.

The chimney is as tall as a high-rise apartment building but considerably narrower, a gigantic tube made from smooth concrete built by a team of Singaporean engineers specializing in the construction of silos, reservoirs, and industrial chimneys. It was their idea to paint it in cheerful, pale colors: two shades of light blue, indigo, sunshine yellow and baby pink cover the entire facade of the svelte building like streamers and confetti.

This giant, festively decorated exhaust pipe would be the centerpiece of this landscape were it not for the power plant itself, a building so large and so purple, it seems to engulf the surrounding circus of hilltops with its imposing presence. The building comprises a row of three blocks clad in sheet metal: three production units generating 800 megawatts apiece. These are linked by aerial walkways, the last of which is still under construction.

This chimney (whose colors I'll later learn from my research were chosen to imitate those of wild lily) has no smoke coming from it as I survey the perimeter of the site, which is largely made up of colossal scaffolding and construction sites that stretch all the way down to the sea. Enclosed behind green fences, there are various types of machinery in operation upon acres of land, creating a soundscape of shrill beeping, humming engines, and the scraping of earth. Occasionally, you can hear the sound of gravel tumbling from the heights of the construction site to the ground in large plastic tubes.

From the fences lining the roadside hang various signs in Chinese, which I try, unsuccessfully, to translate using an app on my phone. As I later learn from the website of the construction site owner, Taipower, they are there to explain that a new terminal will soon be built for the delivery of large volumes of coal to the site.

The sea, now turquoise with the sun at its zenith, is neither beautiful nor inspiring, romantic nor refreshing, vast nor majestic, because there is no one here to look at it in that way. The only people around are busy rearranging the coastline for the industry to exploit. Here, the sea is prosaic, nothing more than a vehicle, the cheapest and most convenient of all. Leaning against the traffic barrier on the freeway (which I have made it a point of honor to walk along), I watch for a while as it crashes into a tiny estuary strewn with detritus, where small white wading birds are scurrying about.

In the space of fifty years, everything has changed in Linkou except for the seasons, and even those have become easier to weather with the introduction of air conditioning. Rapid industrialization, a succession of four-year economic plans, domestic growth, the proliferation of mains-connected electronic devices, the course of history, the ways of the world: all these things have converged, leaving nothing of the little thermal power station that the British engineer came to work on back in 1971.

Nothing, that is, except the authorization to burn coal here for the purposes of energy production. The 300-megawatt English Electric generator was decommissioned in 2014, as was the first unit installed by Westinghouse, each to be replaced by the very latest generation of "ultra-supercritical" turbines supplied by Japanese company Mitsubishi Heavy Industries. These turbines are at least twice as efficient as those of the past, operating at infernal temperatures and pressure levels, virtually without human intervention, thanks to the magic of well-trained algorithms. They are also misleadingly presented as using "clean" coal, when in fact the plants are simply *not as dirty* as their predecessors.

"Taipei? The women will be all over you, they love white men. They're very open over there. Sultry. Submissive but explosive. Reserved but wild. Easy upkeep as long as you don't go bringing one home with you…"

Your colleagues duly acknowledged the news of your expatriation with dirty laughs and racist comments. To this day, Asian women still struggle to disassociate themselves from the specter of the infamous Madame Chrysanthème.

Whatever your initial intentions, misgivings, or principles, it's hard to believe you never took advantage of the flocks of women with no qualifications who, unable to secure employment on weaving machines or electronic device assembly lines, became "girlfriends," masseuses, dancers, or whatever euphemism was used in Taiwan back then. It's hard to imagine that, when leaving the bar on a Friday night with your colleagues, you didn't do precisely what was expected of you, of men your age, from your country, with your purchasing power, which was to drink copious quantities of alcohol in the arms of a girl before screwing her in a shabby room above the bar.

This behavior was more or less a way of conforming to social pressure. Being a white man and not contributing to that economy, not going to the bars to consume women and alcohol alike, was out of the question if you didn't want to be considered a bad guest. When in China, do as the Chinese do, especially since there wasn't really anything to stop you back then, morally (sexual liberation had seen to that) or in terms of health risks (it would be ten years until the arrival of HIV).

Everyone from expats to American privates would frequent the brothels and beaches, and whether they liked it or not, whether they felt bad about it or not, most people ended up thinking it was normal.

These women, some of whom had no shortage of perspicacity, had two categories to distinguish between: on the one hand were the real bastards, the men who had become that way either by natural predisposition or excessive detachment. On the other hand were the sweet guys, the shy guys, the nice guys, the lost souls, the "victims of circumstance" (even though that's hardly the right word, as no man in that situation is ever dispossessed of his free will). Then there were those who were there because they didn't want to refuse an invitation extended by a superior, for example. It was the second category those women often tried to stick with. Perhaps because they knew that if they professed their love, these men would be better clients. Perhaps because love is the word we give to the makeshift agreement between two human beings who are tired of being realists. And so there were times when a "girlfriend" became a regular fixture, an official partner, or even (though much more rarely) a wife under the pretext of love.

Though I can't say for sure, I doubt this was your story. Those women would have used some form of contraception. You arrived in Taipei in 1971, and your first daughter was born in 1972, which means your wife must have fallen pregnant quickly and you must have wanted the child.

Who was she, the mother of your first children? Where did you meet her?

At the infirmary after a work accident, where she slowly changed the bandages of a burn while you closed your eyes and inhaled the sweet smell of her sweat mixed with camphor?

Or perhaps she appeared in the warm lantern light at the night market, at your favorite noodle bar, from the steamy aroma of an enormous pot of broth, wearing a printed silk scarf over hair tied up at the nape of her slender neck.

The most likely scenario is that she was employed on the Linkou construction site as a secretary, assistant, translator, or receptionist. Serving drip coffee, touch typing, her fingers flying over the hammer keys on the typewriter, a Bakelite telephone receiver wedged between her collarbone and ear. Let's be honest: it would have taken you several weeks to be able to pick out her bright and shapely face, made all the more charming by one small, single imperfection, say a chickenpox scar on the side of one nostril. Sometimes your eyes would linger on her ankles, which glistened beneath sheer nylon stockings in winter. Tenderly you observed that fascinating metamorphosis she underwent depending on which language she was speaking: from the timid purr of her soft English, peppered with the nasal inflections of her native tongue that gave her the air of a tender infant, to the Mandarin she projected rapidly like knives onto a moving target, which made her seem strong, not to say a little frightening.

It makes me angry, to put it mildly, to think that you probably reproduced later with my mother what you had first experienced in Taiwan. The idea that you took the liberty of seducing her, with her eminent singularity, her unique qualities, and even allowed yourself to believe that you loved her, exactly as you had loved the woman before her—the other Asian woman.

Deep down, I would rather have discovered that the woman you married in Taiwan was a former prostitute who used a timely pregnancy to worm her way into your life. If I were to truly grant myself all the license I claim to in writing about your life, I would characterize the marriage as forced by guilt, accidental, compromised by dubious beginnings, and doomed to eternal bitterness. But I suppose, at this point at least, I still have too much respect for reality.

I EVALUATE EVERY building I see (this one too new, that one too tall) and by process of elimination, I draw him a background (more modest here, less cluttered there). In certain areas, in the districts that appear to predate capitalist development, I imagine the places he might have walked: around the corner of a particular garden, past this statue, this chaotic pile of mopeds, amongst the stalls of a covered market, at the top of a street where people have been selling sculpted jade since the beginning of time. At a crossroads amongst a flurry of night owls, beneath the archway of a building with a tiled facade. Perhaps he pushed open this door, perhaps the sign was already flashing above it back then. That could once have been him, the long silhouette under the neon light, bursting through the cast-aluminum door towards a mysterious interior at the top of a narrow staircase.

In the back room of a little restaurant specializing in spicy duck stew, I sit face-to-face with a flat-screen television that is almost exclusively showing advertisements for air conditioning units, occasionally interrupted by snippets of variety shows featuring women singing and dancing in glittery dresses. In an attempt to keep warm despite the fact that it's thirty-two degrees outside, I choose the only table in the restaurant that isn't directly beneath an air conditioning unit (there are four, one on each wall running on full blast, plus a ceiling fan that is turning in vain).

There must have been evenings when he sat just like me, alone in the back room of a joint like this, setting his tastebuds on fire with red chili. Back in the days before air conditioning, he was probably sweating profusely, cursing the climate here, perhaps proclaiming his undying love for the cold and damp of his Welsh island to anyone who would listen.

In another life, maybe, we could have laughed about it together.

Whenever I travel this part of the world, I find myself readily (and hypocritically) cursing the omnipresence of air conditioning. After all, what Taiwanese person on a visit to Europe would be so arrogant as to complain about the excess of radiators preventing them from enjoying the temperate climate they've been dreaming of all year?

But aside from having a personal preference for hot, tropical climates, I think there's something objectively frightening about the rampant proliferation of air conditioning units, as with electronic devices. I once decided to count the appliances in my own apartment: twenty-eight lamps, nine radiators, a fan-assisted oven, a microwave, a four-burner stove, a toaster, a kettle, a rice cooker, a mixer, a juice extractor, an induction milk emulsifier, a raclette machine, a yogurt maker, three radios, a vacuum cleaner, three computers, a stereo system, a video projector, one music and one video streaming device, four mini-speakers, one of which is wireless, two pairs of rechargeable headphones, a Wi-Fi modem, a tablet, four cell phones, three electric toothbrushes, and five faucets that run hot water, all of which is more or less average in households like mine, made up of two adults and two children.

Bearing in mind that my way of life is one aspired to by billions of people who do not yet have the same purchasing power, how can we for a second believe that "clean" coal sold as a transitional alternative to nuclear energy will do anything more than simply absorb the increase in electricity consumption that will inevitably come from global demographic growth? How can we imagine, or even hope, that the four hundred and forty-four active nuclear reactors in the world will be replaced, instantly and at any cost, by just as many if not more coal chimneys? Because even if they're painted the colors of wild lilies and equipped with the best particle filters, this will inevitably result in an increase in carbon dioxide in the atmosphere. Yet given that solar and wind energy are, to my knowledge, currently unable to effectively compensate for the closure of a nuclear power plant, any anti-nuclear policies that are not coupled with the kinds of radical restrictive measures no politician dares take to reduce energy consumption will necessarily lead to a systematic increase in respiratory and pulmonary diseases accompanied by dangerous climate disruption.

In this sense, the proliferation of air conditioning units is cause for concern indeed. Sometimes, when I run the dishwasher, I wonder whether, when we made household appliances available to all, we irrevocably triggered the beginning of the end of the world.

AT SUNSET, the rice paddies, vast reflective patches of water, would blaze in unison with the sky like a mosaic of mirrors turning amber to crimson from one second to the next. On the horizon, the paper cutout of mountains appeared darker than the night sky, and far beyond them, you could see the sparse, flickering constellation of the city. From the roof terrace of your building, you had a carpet of rice paddies as a substitute sea view.

In the backdrop I've given you for your new, domestic life, I've built a small building with tiled facades, a balcony fully enclosed by a wire screen and large, sliding, triple-paned windows. Your apartment is fitted out with varnished bamboo and faux-leather furniture and has three rooms for you to walk in and out of wearing a silk bathrobe in the summer, barefoot on the pale, checkered parquet.

By this time your wife, once radiant and well-dressed, had now become a silhouette fading away behind the newborn baby she never put down. It wasn't so long ago that you loved that body, still smooth and fleshy, strong and muscular, hairless, slightly clammy, and perfumed. You had used and abused it for your own pleasure under the illusion that it was your plaything, a toy that was now no longer yours. The small, shapeless infant that had just burst forth from that body continued to monopolize it.

Like many other fathers before you, you lived through the birth of your first child in the shame of your own jealousy. Far from any metaphysical giddiness or dignified emotions—which at any rate, society did not expect from men back then—you struggled with a feeling of injustice you had to keep to yourself.

The baby's wailing split your head in two, and seeing her, your wife, become the ardent slave to those bestial calls made you dream of escaping that atmosphere saturated with odors and cries.

Luckily, your wife was Chinese and your era was one of sexual liberation, which granted you, for a time—from the last months of pregnancy, through breastfeeding, to the return of her periods—the liberty to have sex with other women without anyone batting an eyelid. After spending your days onsite at Linkou, scheduling tests, ordering parts, writing telexes to headquarters, planning shifts, spending your days in a hard hat and overalls amidst the rumbling racket of machines, supervising crane maneuvers and the ballet of forklift trucks and hoists, you'd head to the bar with your colleagues, only returning well into the night once everyone was asleep.

In a little room adjacent to your bedroom, your wife had placed a mattress on the floor where she would sleep, practically naked, with her child. In the living room, your mother-in-law, who was now living with you, had set up her bed between the sofa and the sliding balcony door that opened up onto the mosquito net. Outside, the night crackled with life, interspersed now and then with the distant sound of a motor racing down an adjacent road.

You'd open the fridge, not to take anything out, but to enjoy a flash of white cold and the faint aroma of daikon radish, before going to sleep alone in your bedroom, on the large, mahogany bed frame with a slatted base and tall legs complete with the mattress you had imported from Europe. On the bedroom table, a digital clock displayed the hours and minutes in green, separated by two blinking dots that marked the passage of each second, countless yet fleeting, before another identical day began. Tomorrow would be the same as yesterday, over and over again.

A life void of any spark or grandeur, comfortable and mediocre, exotic and bourgeois. A life earning a living in the prestigious machine industry, a bohemian fatherhood in a developing Asian country, which you never really planned or chose. This life was yours now.

KORI

TEN YEARS HAVE passed and the entrance to the port of Busan has changed beyond recognition. This country truly is moving too fast. Since my last visit, the container ship terminal, or at least the bulk of its activities, has been moved a couple of dozen miles to better accommodate the inexorable increase in the number of objects in circulation around the world: large or small, simple or complex, cheap or expensive, packaged or loose, useful or frivolous. The terminal now appears on satellite images to the right of the entrance to Jinhae Bay, to the west of the estuary of the Nakdong River, a blue and red checkerboard of containers in tightly packed rows on a rectangular strip of concrete creeping its way up the mountain and into the sea. The powerful mechanical beasts these infrastructures are designed to accommodate enter beneath a brand-new bridge some five miles in length, passing on their way a cluster of practically deserted islets. Having never taken this route, I've never seen these islets in real life, but you can make out their beauty even from a map: scraps of rock coiffed with curly vegetation, immersed in perilous waters.

Ten years prior, for my own pleasure, I'd boarded a container ship in Fos-sur-Mer and traveled half the world before the ship came in, not via these modern infrastructures, but the historic port of Busan on a winter morning. The rain had come to unburden the humid air and every inch of the landscape was a reflection of the triumphant sun. I remember the scene as a goldsmith's painting, the city a sparkling mosaic tumbling down a hillside.

There's nothing like arriving in a city by boat: the shiver it sends down your spine, the contraction of every abdominal muscle, your racing heart a counterpoint to the slow, solemn rhythm of the heavy vessel. Bridges go by, the city's buildings form a guard of honor, and you forget for a moment whether the city or the vessel is the one in motion. As you arrive, you discover a face of the metropolis that can never be seen from dry land.

After twenty-eight days at sea, I was moved by the arrival of the container ship, which, like me, was returning to the city of its birth, flying a courtesy flag, the South-Korean Taegeukgi. The gargantuan vessel had been ordered by the French from Samsung Heavy Industries shipyards a few years prior, at a time when trade between Europe and Asia seemed destined for eternal exponential growth.

Back then, I knew nothing about the man I am inventing in these pages. Knowing he had been a sailor might have made me think fondly of him, prone as I am to the romanticism of the sea. But I didn't need him to fall in love with boats.

At the time of writing, I haven't been back to Busan, now a memory a decade old.

My mother and I lived not far from Haeundae beach, in an apartment he visited occasionally and apparently even lived in for a while. Having disembarked from my container ship, I went to revisit the little apartment block where the scenes of family life captured in my baby photo album had played out, if for only a little while: portrait of the baby in its crib with sky-blue nylon bedding, joyous bath time in a tub of lukewarm water, mother and baby in a rattan rocking chair, outings in a stroller (modern equipment par excellence at a time when Korean mothers still carried their infants around on their backs in slings), a curious crowd of neighborhood children looking at the strange, round-eyed infant in a lace bonnet, the Western baby that came out of a Korean belly.

This district, which sprung up from the ground in the '70s thanks to American development aid, was the height of modernity. When I arrived after my long trip at sea, I photographed those faded yellow and ocher facades, the grills covering the ground-floor windows, the little square balconies that are no longer constructed for modern high-rise apartment buildings, the glass doors with aluminum handles. I walked around the rusted playgrounds that were brightly colored in the pictures from my childhood.

I learned from an aunt who still lives in Busan that those little five-floor buildings were recently destroyed to be replaced by tower blocks at least four times the size. The buildings would feature apartments containing multiple refrigerators with ice dispensers, giant, flat-screen televisions, and ultra-powerful air conditioning units (in South Korea, the country of industrial conglomerates, the property developers and white goods manufacturers are sometimes one and the same).

WHAT WAS YOUR state of mind, what kind of mental arrangement had you made with yourself that gave you the gall to smile at my mother as she stood behind the camera, photographing you in a brown tracksuit in the apartment in Haeundae, holding the child she had just given birth to? Those two little girls you'd fathered were in Taipei with their mother while you struck a relaxed, paternal pose, holding a baby you would never acknowledge.

Having landed in Asia a single man, how did you deal with finding yourself, six years later, the father of three children by two different women in two different developing countries? How were you hoping to reconcile those two buds of the same family tree, if not by acknowledging paternity, then in terms of moral responsibility? Leave one for the other? Abandon the second to stay with the first? Or why not live as a polygamist? After all, that would have been the most pragmatic way to economically secure the future of all those women and girls.

Surely you would have found a solution. Your world, your era, was one of optimism and confidence in the future. People were making babies in the same way they were building nuclear power plants, persuading themselves that, since the best was yet to come, solutions would eventually be found to the problems they were choosing not to see.

It was in that photo of us together, the baby and her genitor, that I first saw your face. I discovered it later in life, well into my thirties, in a box of old pictures belonging to my mother. Those images had been relegated to the back of a cupboard, never to grace the official family albums. I stood there for a long time, speechless, looking at a face so undeniably similar to my own. It's a dizzying sensation, to discover as an adult such an obvious resemblance between yourself and a complete stranger.

The image has now been left to lie, relegated once more—and perhaps destined to forever remain—between the pages of an English poetry anthology you gave to my mother.

You liked gifting books and you liked poetry. The book and its faded cover, after various moves and a fairly solemn bequest, has finally ended up in my library, in the dustiest and most inaccessible corner.

It was like a scene from a film, though neither my mother nor I had anticipated having the conversation. In her kitchen one afternoon in 2009, we set about making mandu together, a kind of Korean dumpling that I particularly like to eat around the time of Lunar New Year, in a soup called tteok mandu guk, literally "rice cake and dumpling soup." We had never cooked together, and we never have since. But both of us, she then I, had just read a book by Shin Kyung-sook entitled *Please Look After Mother*. The book is set in post-war South Korea during those years when the women and men of the country felt as though they had been requisitioned, almost mobilized, to get the national economy off the ground as quickly as possible. As always, when I'm plunged back into South Korea by a book or a film, I was gripped by a burning desire to eat its food, a way of metabolizing the singular culture that is only tangentially my own. So I suggested making mandu together, and as we did, I began to ask her about her childhood, then her experience of entering the South Korean workforce towards the end of the 1960s. She spoke of a country where families were large, resources were limited, and parental decisions were guided by Confucian tradition: boys were sent off to study, girls were destined to marry. And since marriage meant servitude to the husband's family, education was naturally denied to girls, as it was considered a wasted investment. My mother was the fourth of eight children. All of her brothers studied. She was deprived of an education. But being curious and persevering as she was, she learned English almost entirely by teaching herself. Armed with this significant advantage in a country where many Western companies were still securing long-term contracts, she forged herself a career path that took her far from the mediocre existence her feminine condition had destined her for.

We both had our hands in the raw mandu stuffing when she reached the part in her story about working for GEC Turbine Generators, a British company that had come to equip the Kori nuclear power plant. That's when she began telling me about her encounter with my biological father. After the conversation—which I won't recount here because it has since been wiped from my memory for reasons a psychologist would likely be able to explain—we took the dumplings, all neatly folded into half-moons, sealed them in airtight boxes, and my mother went to fetch the book of poetry for me. On a square Post-it, she'd written the names of a few colleagues from that time and assured me that I would have both her and my father's support, should I ever feel the urge to go in search of my genitor.

It took almost ten years, and the pretext of this book, for me to decide to set out on that journey.

KORI WAS A small fishing village like so many others along that stretch of Korean coastline, until the neighboring megalopolis extended its long, tarmac tentacles and annexed them. There were just short of one hundred and fifty houses and almost as many boats moored in a tiny bay with its back to the Taebaek mountains, facing the East Sea.

In 1968, when the villagers saw a convoy of official cars appear full of men from the city, some in suits and ties, others in high grade military uniforms, they saw no cause for concern. The villagers in their traditional unbleached clothing (crossed over at the front, tight around the ankles), whose opinions did not count for anything in the inexorable march of progress, remained largely indifferent to the presence of these bigwigs bustling around. Perhaps the less impassive among them even welcomed the central government taking an interest in their little community.

The delegations came one after the other, often accompanied by one or two Westerners who could be spotted a mile off by their fair hair and tall stature. Soon, it was announced that a nuclear power plant was to be built there: a factory, an abstraction, from which electricity would flow. But for the site to be built, the village would have to be razed to the ground. Everyone would be rehoused, of course, the men in ties had promised. And new houses would be constructed not far from the bay, modern, heated buildings connected at the source to this prodigious energy. At the entrance to the nuclear power station, a plaque would be mounted to thank the one thousand two hundred and fifty historical inhabitants of Kori for the sacrifice they were going to agree to make for the good of the nation.

Had they ever known what it was like to be connected to the grid? The division of the country after the war in 1953 cut South Korea off from its only functional domestic sources of energy: a few hydroelectric power plants, all in the 38th parallel north. The North is also where the few remaining factories built under Japanese occupation were located. The South had only really ever had fishing, livestock farming, and agriculture since the dawn of time. They used candles for light. They used wood for heating. Winters were terribly cold, terribly dark, and newborns and the elderly often perished.

A nuclear power plant—what could that possibly mean? The process would potentially bring employment: easier jobs for the sons of the sea, jobs less subject to the whims of the sky, jobs of an unprecedented kind that could be done sitting down and would extend life expectancy. Above all, the whole country would have access to an extraordinary amount of electricity, which would light up the streets and houses, power machines they could only dream of, and bring the Republic of Korea into the closed circle of nuclear powers. Thanks to foreign technologies, bought ready for use from the Americans in exchange for allegiance to free-market capitalism, South Korea was about to take its revenge on history, revenge for the misery of war and the injustices of Japanese colonialism.

SIPPING ON A white coffee in the bay window of an ultra-modern coffee shop, I look out through a light veil of fog at the first four domes of the Kori nuclear power plant. The barista has drawn a flower in the froth. Everywhere I look, South Korea's vengeance for the war and colonialism resembles the glossy pages of an architecture magazine, only pushed to the point of absurdity. This small, asymmetrical building seems to take itself for Casa Malaparte (only built on the side of the highway, in true South Korean property speculation fashion) with its spare, contemporary furnishings, clever use of glass, succulents, and a view of the sea, all of which provide a backdrop for men and women dressed like nowhere else taking their selfies, social climbers who watch themselves exist through small, backlit touchscreens. This village, flanked by two different expressions of reinforced concrete, could tell the entire contemporary history of the Republic of Korea. On one side, a 6,000-megawatt nuclear power plant complex, on the other, spectacular tourist infrastructures reserved for glampers. In less than half a century, South Korea went from thirty million inhabitants subsisting on very little, to fifty-one million consumers thriving in the world's eleventh-largest economy.

A short but necessary digression on glamping: the term is a portmanteau of "glamorous" and "camping" and refers to a category of tourist accommodation for bohemian aesthetes that seems to be gaining popularity among the upper-middle classes and countries seeking Instagrammable leisure activities. Glamping can either mean large, luxurious tents fitted out in a romantic style, evoking the heyday of the British Empire (the kind of nomadic set up that would once have been erected with the help of slaves) or, as is the case in Kori, retro camper vans. Not the large white caravans driven along the freeway by ruddy-faced holiday makers, but sophisticated mobile homes that borrow from the 1960s American aesthetic in pale pink, turquoise, or cream, each featuring Formica interiors that have been carefully restored to discreetly incorporate everything the discerning traveler expects from upmarket accommodation (Wi-Fi connection and a selection of organic, Ayurvedic teas). The tents and caravans are situated a stone's throw away from shared toilets (whose only factor distinguishing them from five-star hotel toilets is precisely the fact that they are shared), and close to bars and restaurants with the same target market: in this case a glass and concrete construction, home to a chic coffee shop serving cheesecakes and latte macchiato around the clock (literally any time, day or night). Having insufficiently planned for my trip, I ended up staying in one of these caravans, a mid-range model, by chance and for one night only, as the glamping facilities were fully booked over the following days. From this rocky black promontory, amidst large, knotty tree trunks and the scent of local pine, there's a panoramic view of a fishing port and a gray sea flecked white by gusts of wind. There, on the other side of the bay, at the far end of a hill that sticks out like a tongue into the sea, the nuclear power plant I like to think of as my birthplace appears like a cluster of barnacles on the tail fin of some great sea mammal.

IN THE SPACE that is still occupied by the first Kori reactor to this day, there was once a bongsudae, a cylindrical stone construction that served as a kind of rudimentary lighthouse. From the tops of the ridges and peaks of this mountainous country, these were used to warn inhabitants of military emergencies, for example, using smoke or fire to send an alert far and wide. In my image of Korea, which oscillates between sixteenth century silk paintings and contemporary ultra-HD modern cinema, the flame of these buildings is fanned by villagers in off-white clothing carrying bundles of sticks on their backs using a traditional tool known as a jige. This ingenious thing about the jige, a wooden device with straps made from braided straw, is that it can be supported by a large retractable stand for resting or unloading, so the person carrying it never has to bend down. Elderly generations in the mountain regions still use the jige to this day for transporting heavy loads such as kindling for subfloor heating in some rustic houses. In Korea, you only need to go back one or two generations to find relics of the Middle Ages.

The first Kori reactor was built on a natural promontory, one of the points in the topography that catches the eye, a spot from which you can see and be seen from far and wide. Facing out towards the sea and the eyes of the world like an ancient bongsudae, the first nuclear power plant on the Korean peninsula was sending a signal of its own.

There are two television archives that provide a good summary of that period. The first is from 1971. The black-and-white footage shows the President of the Republic of Korea addressing a vast audience of villagers sitting cross-legged on the bare ground, knee-to-knee, in their coarse traditional clothing. Faces of men wearing wide-brimmed cylindrical hats, some with a wisp of beard like lace on their chins; faces of women with broad cheeks framed by scarves tied at the neck. Behind them, the second row of the crowd is standing, wearing business clothes teamed with canes and long coats. They are standing to avoid getting dirty, standing because their Western clothing indicates they embrace progress, standing because those clothes were not designed for sitting cross-legged in the traditional way.

Addressing them from a rectangular stage protected from the sun by a small wooden building, the president is flanked by two tight rows of officials. One month later to the day (the footage is dated March 27), a presidential election will be held, which for once will be genuinely contested in this pseudo-parliamentary democracy, led for nine years by a former army general.

At the end of a relatively brief speech, in which science and technology are evoked like fairy godmothers at the cradle of this great nation, the president presses a detonator, and a stick of dynamite explodes a few dozen feet away, at the exact spot where the concrete will be poured in preparation for South Korea's first nuclear reactor. (For maximum symbolic impact, the dynamite could obviously have been placed inside the old bongsudae for this political spectacle, but there is no evidence to suggest that this was the case.)
One month later, the president, General Park Chung-hee, would win the election that put his post on the line. He declared martial law shortly afterwards and was president for what was to be the rest of his life, because eight years later, while still in power, he was assassinated.

During that time, he was responsible for the famous "Miracle on the Han River," a period of spectacular economic growth that would be held up as a model for global financial institutions, notwithstanding that the miracle owed its existence to an equally spectacular suppression of civil rights. Running water, electricity… and widespread surveillance. The government was transforming US economic aid into industrial power with one hand, and repressing any form of dissidence through torture with the other.

Eight years, or just under, is also the time it would take to build and commission the first of the four nuclear reactors included in the ten-year investment program.

The second archive video, dated 1978, shows the same president, this time in color, wearing a pin-striped suit and a strange sort of Panama hat that make him look like a godfather in the Mafia. In his buttonhole, he is wearing not just a single flower, but an entire floral arrangement. The officials surrounding him, meanwhile, are sporting large medals with thick yellow ribbons of the sort usually reserved for adorning the winning animals at an agricultural show (at least, that's the only place I have ever come across such a thing). In front of him, in lieu of the chaotic hodgepodge of cross-legged villagers in the first video, soldiers and workers in uniform have been organized in lines and are standing to attention.

Following a speech on the importance of science and technology for bolstering national prosperity, Park Chung-hee once again sets off the dynamite, this time in the spot where the second Kori nuclear reactor will be built. Then he goes off to visit the first reactor, which has just been connected to the grid, surrounded by his large delegation of men in suits, ties, and ribbons.

The very same day, July 21, a few miles south of the spectacle, a tiny girl wearing an odd little lace bonnet was taking her first steps in the dirt of a colorful playground in front of the barred windows of a yellow and ocher building under the watchful eye of an aunt or neighbor.

Her mother had started a new job and met new colleagues, but perhaps she still found herself crying from time to time, because the man she wanted to love could not find it in himself to give her anything more than poetry books.

I COULD HAVE asked my mother questions, but I prefer to make it all up myself.

This way, perhaps, under the guise of fiction, swaddled in my imagination, my mother will be better protected. Another person who will be protected is the tall, shy, and skinny young man she fell in love with a few years after I was born. The man she followed to Europe. The man who became the only father I know.

Fiction, I told myself, will provide each of us, in the family triangle we've forged over the past forty years, with our own retreat, our own refuge in its shadows. Fiction will preserve the silences in each of our respective histories that have become more constituent than words.

And besides, this act of inventing, embroidering, dimming the light, blurring the contours, closing your eyes, dreaming up your own origins—isn't this the strategy all children have for escaping their parents?

HER DESK WAS always tidy and decorated with flowers. As she entered the building of gray, beige, and lifeless blue, she would hang up her fire-red coat. She sat at her desk, her shapely face lit up on the left-hand side by a small window with an aluminum frame that let in a cold draft in winter, the dust in summer. She had all the elegance of a queen, sitting there, back straight, at the far end of a room her colleagues would have to cross if they wanted to assign her a task, make a request, hand in a report, or ask her a question. All around her, like hundreds of notes being played in the silence, the metallic clatter of nimble fingers on typewriter keys; a single, sharp, high-pitched chime at the end of every line. Covering the walls were maps and numbered diagrams, technical line drawings depicting cross sections of machines in black ink. Alongside them, calendars covered with scribbles, including one featuring England's most beautiful monuments. Often, she would lose herself in those images, and she privately swore to visit all of those places one day. Outside, the sounds of the construction site, the constant whirring of motors, the smell of burnt diesel. Often, the sky was hazy.

You never went to the parties your younger colleagues organized to ward off the boredom of life on the site. Saturday night parties full of people laughing loudly and listening to records, happily crammed into makeshift rooms with orange wallpaper and postcards tacked to the walls. Parties where people pushed furniture aside to sit on the floor between overflowing ashtrays, using their lighters to uncap pale, lightly bitter Korean beers and drinking straight from the bottle. You were ten years older than most of the other expats. You were an executive. And you were married.

She enjoyed the simple, smiling company of these young Europeans, their broken English, and the playfulness of the temporary social ties they were developing here, far away from home. With them, she was able to escape the rigidity and social hierarchies of her country. With them she was free, she was their equal, while in the eyes of her compatriots and her family she was just a woman, which is to say nothing, or worse.

You started to notice her interest for unusual English expressions, a desire to fill in the gaps in her knowledge of the language she worked in. The way she would tilt her head and furrow her eyebrows ever so slightly to show that she had identified an inconsistency, a potential problem, a flaw in the line of reasoning. She was the most reliable of all the girls who worked in that drafty shack. Not only was she beautiful and joyful, she strove for excellence with a passion that was far from naive for a career she didn't find alienating. She wanted to learn, she wanted to progress, because progress would make her free. In a way, the Anglo-American management style imported alongside these new megatechnologies represented just that: the possibility of changing one's lot in life through merit. Her mastery of a foreign language had opened up unexpected vistas, introducing her to ideas that had not yet been instilled in Korea. Democracy. Freedom of expression. Feminism. Once that window had been opened, there was no going back. She worked to achieve a level of excellence that might one day enable her to escape somewhere far away. She seemed to exude a certain sort of idealism.

You kept your distance with her and everyone else on site, which was put down to your position of authority. It just so happened that being in that part of the world, at that time, amongst those people, automatically gave you an air of mystery, one you made no effort to dispel.

She watched you each day, making decisions, settling matters, saying yes, giving your approval, or conversely, sending plans back, getting angry, being annoyed by the things being imposed upon you by headquarters and subcontractors. Your work, which had once been purely technical, had now become political. Everything had to be discussed, negotiated, analyzed. You had to play it safe, there was very little leeway, and all the while you kept a relatively calm aura of charisma that was rather becoming. You were tall, your hair fell in fine curls that were starting to turn gray. You were so different from all those Korean men she'd seen in similar roles. You weren't authoritarian or bad-tempered with the people around you. You didn't have that violence in you. And though she never thought of it as such, because back then love wasn't analyzed the way it is today, those were the things that won her over. Then one evening, you asked her out to dinner.

Forty years later, my mother would not recognize herself in the young woman she once was. She didn't have the same compulsions or the same restraint. She would think that woman naive, a little embarrassing. Perhaps she would even want to shake her, tell her to wake up, fight for her with the weapons only time and experience can arm us with.

But given the circumstances, given the cruelty of her country, now difficult to imagine, that young woman demonstrated remarkable pugnacity. The proof is in her smile in photos from that time, a smile that grew broader once she arrived in Europe.

And besides, did she really need to be protected from herself? Wouldn't that erase the history that, for better or worse, has now become ours?

LESS THAN TWO years after South Korea stated its intention to phase out nuclear, the country launched its twenty-sixth reactor, a stone's throw away from the one that had just been shut down. Economic realism drives politicians to lie continually. Within forty years, South Korea had become one of the most competitive exporters of nuclear technology in the world. Nowhere else on the planet did the decision to phase out nuclear feel so contradictory, so paradoxical. It seemed to fly in the face of the only true power governing the world: the capitalist economy.

Having already purchased around a dozen ready-for-use nuclear power plants from abroad, South Korea began to build its own pressurized water reactors in the 1980s, the plans for which it took from a US contract that permitted technology transfer.

In this respect, the Three Mile Island incident in 1979 came just at the right time to serve South Korea's ambitions: when the government of Chun Doo-hwan, another autocrat with a military background, issued a call for tenders, the entire commercial nuclear industry was at a standstill. It had been paralyzed by public opinion, which was now up in arms against "nuclear," a singular noun that refers, in no particular order, to arsenals of weapons of mass destruction, atomic-powered submarines and electricity-generating plants. "Nuclear" had become synonymous with "toxic," and people were generally "against nuclear," in the same way they were "against global famine." After Three Mile Island, the whole industry knew it would take years for electricity producers in Europe and the United States to start reinvesting in anything besides gas and coal.

Combustion Engineering, a manufacturer of pressurized water reactors based in Connecticut, decided that a South Korean contract with a ten-year technology transfer was a good way to tide them over until bankruptcy.[1] And so it was that the South Koreans patiently and quietly set about developing their own commercial nuclear expertise, first learning to tame this foreign technology, before upgrading it to greater capacities, while the rest of the world's nuclear industry was mired in a crisis commensurate with the hubris that had propelled it to that point in the first place.

Over the last five years of the twentieth century, the first South Korean OPR-1000 reactors were connected to the electricity grid. Twenty years later came the APR-1400, a more advanced version. These two models belong to a family of machines that can now be found all over the world, akin

[1] Combustion Engineering was bought out by ABB in 1990, then sold to Alstom, and later to Westinghouse when the latter was still owned by British Nuclear Fuels, which was eventually sold to Toshiba before it went bankrupt in 2017.

to those found in France, for example, to this day. Technical side note: in these pressurized water reactors, the nuclear reactor core is not immersed in graphite as is the case with its magnox counterparts, but in water, which slows down the neutrons and cools the core. The nuclear fuel is assembled in the same rods made of "enriched" uranium, i.e. uranium to which fissile material (U235) has been added to make it more reactive. The steam that drives the generating turbines comes from a second water circuit, which is completely separate from the first and therefore never comes into contact with any radioactive elements.

Curiously, when it came to nuclear power, South Korea chose not to follow in the footsteps of Great Britain and the United States, for what may have been the only time in its modern history, by choosing not to leave the free market to its own devices. With the country technically still at war and under the thumb of a military general, a decision was made to follow France's lead and stake everything on centralized standardization. This strategy consisted of investing in one single technology, gaining intimate knowledge of its inner workings, strengths, and weaknesses, then training battalions of engineers to become experts in it, before replicating the same product across the whole country. A single, state-owned company divided into different units would then oversee the entire integrated industry under a single brand name, designing, purchasing, planning, building, maintaining and repairing the whole country's electro-nuclear equipment. (It is worth noting that this market concentration also enabled the vast system of corruption that came to light in 2011. For years, corrupt officials authorized the purchase and installation of a large number of counterfeit parts. Several nuclear plants had to be closed consecutively across the peninsula for the preventative replacement of all the non-conforming parts.)

South Korean reactors enjoy an excellent technical reputation and win international tenders today (at the expense of France in particular), which is perhaps due to the fact that this vertical, centralized organization is underpinned in the country by endemic Confucianism. When applied to the construction and management of nuclear power plants, a collective sense of purpose, coupled with obedience, subservience, and the repression of all critical thinking required by this philosophy appears to yield excellent results. Because this kind of hyper-complex machinery, like any product of military engineering, requires the human beings working on its deployment to be as reliable as cogs in a machine; it requires them to carry out instructions from above without much thought, without taking the slightest personal initiative, with no room for creative maneuver. After all, you wouldn't want a group of free thinkers to run an aircraft carrier or a submarine, so you certainly wouldn't want them to run a nuclear power plant.

At the end of the day, maybe the success of an electro-nuclear industry is more of a cultural matter than we think.

When I was three, I had a South Korean passport for a few months. This would never have happened had it not been for a young man from Switzerland, temporarily expatriated in South Korea, who fell in love with my mother and sent a letter to her country's authorities, committing to take her as his wife within a reasonable period upon arrival in his own country. It was on this condition alone that my mother and I were authorized to leave South Korea and were each granted a passport for this purpose. On the document, I was assigned my mother's surname and the Korean name she had chosen for me at birth, in the customary order in regions of Chinese-Confucian influence: Lee Hye-rin.

This was not the identity my mother had wanted for me. In my first photo album, she wrote down the time and date of my birth, my weight, the above Korean name followed by a second name in English, and finally, the surname of my genitor, in the customary Western form: Hye-rin Jennifer Ball.

When we arrived in Switzerland, my mother's young fiancé kept his promise. He married her and went immediately afterwards to acknowledge me as his own child. Doing so meant he was required by law to provide for my education and basic material needs. In fact, he went far beyond this minimum legal requirement, ensuring my emotional security, social wellbeing, and the development of my intellectual curiosity, offering me all the material needs I could imagine. Later, he also committed unstintingly to his role as a grandfather: all paternal attributes that make him, indisputably, the only father I recognize.

At the same time, he passed on to my mother and I all the privileges and obligations incumbent on nationals of the small confederation we were about to settle in. It was then that we officially became Swiss citizens of the town of Vuippens, in the canton of Fribourg (a commune that would be absorbed a few decades later by the neighboring commune of Marsens, and that neither my mother nor I, nor the young man who had suddenly become a husband and father all at once, had ever set foot in).

Having duly ceded the responsibility of our social and economic future to Switzerland, the Republic of Korea, which to this day takes pride in the ethnic homogeneity of its population and does not grant its citizens dual nationality, did not hesitate to strip us of our passports, documents that had only been issued to us on the condition we later renounce them.

It was on my new passport, red with a white cross, that I was officially given my surname: the name of my father.

My parents decided, whether by choice or as a result of being pressured, to change the name to make it easier to read and write in French and English (the latter being our lingua franca at the time).

Was this at the benevolent suggestion of an administrative employee, whose cultural horizon was so limited that he could not imagine writing, on such a beautiful passport, a name that was so poorly in keeping with his idea of what citizenship in his country meant? Whatever the case, if my parents' hope was to save me from having to spell out my name, systematically repeat it, or constantly explain its origins, it is clear today that their decision—a compromise that consisted of using the diminutive of the Korean name on my passport—failed to meet its objective by a long stretch. I have spent my entire life trying to explain this strange name. (To think there are people in life who, when they introduce themselves, are able to say: "Hi, I'm Martin," and that's all there is to it.)

I have only ever had a relative, if not fluid, notion of identity. Whether given, acquired, gained or lost, names and passports are transitory, arbitrary and insignificant.

It's clear to me, especially given my personal experience, that identity is never anything more than the byproduct of one or more love affairs. It's a vast field of questions to be plowed, a field sown with doubt, a place where nothing lasting can ever grow.

But we each have a life we never lived, one that evaporates the moment the railroad switch of fate is flicked to one set of tracks rather than another, a shadow that forever looms in the air like a stillborn twin, our own personal Schrödinger's cat. Had I kept the identity I was given at birth, what kind of woman, what kind of mother, what kind of daughter would Jennifer Ball have been?

MONROE

THEY SAY NUCLEAR accidents are caused by a chain of tiny things: faulty valves, malfunctioning indicators, minor design flaws that have long gone unnoticed, individual and collective errors, ignorance and haste.

In movies, we see a close-up of the tense, perspiring faces of men in uniform, compulsively turning the pages of large procedure manuals as warning lights begin to flash one after another, then all at once, until finally an alarm punctuates the silence with its wailing.

Over the course of the sixty years that make up the history of commercial nuclear power, there has been only one occasion on which an earthquake registering 9 on the Richter scale triggered a tsunami that swamped the emergency generators of a nuclear power plant, a scenario that was not covered in the instruction manuals at General Electric (the manufacturers of Reactors 1 and 2 at Fukushima Daiichi).

But aside from this horrifying case, where events took on proportions far surpassing a few operators breaking out in cold sweats, all other nuclear accidents and incidents have been due to a greater or lesser extent to significant human error, poorly executed handovers, and unspoken questions requiring categorical answers. These, when combined with errors of judgment and personal interpretation, can result in the unexpected collapse of a balance even if it has been tried and tested by many a brain and many a calculation.

At Three Mile Island, an electro-nuclear center in Pennsylvania, a gauge on the control room dashboard indicated that a valve in the second reactor was closed, even though it was open. Operators acted accordingly, and blindly—because it's important to remember that you can't see what's going on inside a nuclear reactor, you only ever receive signals transmitted by sensors—and the core partially melted, leading to the evacuation of over one hundred thousand people (for a few days only; afterwards, they all returned home, lived happily, and did not suffer cancer rates any higher than the global average). This occurred in March 1979, and to this day it is still considered to be the worst nuclear accident in American history. But it was not the first. Nor the last.

Seven years prior, in June 1966, in the control room of the Enrico Fermi breeder reactor situated a few hundred yards from Detroit, Michigan, two gauges began to indicate abnormally high temperatures in one part of the core for no apparent reason. Rather than shutting everything down to ascertain the source of this abnormality (as this would be an expensive strategy), the operators simply decided to believe that the temperature sensors must be faulty. But inside the large, windowless containment vessel, there were in fact several elements that were not in their usual places, as gauges linked to other sensors confirmed. Still, at this stage, it seemed perfectly reasonable at all levels of the decision-making chain to do nothing. In hindsight, of course, this is extremely concerning. But it bears repeating that this is largely what industrial accidents are caused by: terrible decisions.

For several months (it's tempting to add one or several exclamation points here), the control panel continued to indicate abnormalities, but the consensus was to simply ignore them. The problem had to be coming from the sensors, not what they were measuring. Finally, one night in October, an alarm signal sounded due to abnormally high levels of radiation inside the reactor, and an emergency shutdown had to be performed.

Unsurprisingly, the investigation revealed that the temperature sensors were perfectly functional. A piece of metal from a poorly welded safety device had come loose inside the reactor vessel, preventing the liquid sodium (used for cooling) from reaching some of the fuel rods.

There was a rumor widely spread in the media that the piece of metal was in fact a beer can left in the bottom of the tank by a careless worker. It's difficult to decide whether this simplistic fantasy is more or less bleak than the reality.

Whatever the case, luckily—and this is not just a turn of phrase, seeing as the fortuitous outcome is in no part thanks to human intervention—all the radioactive material slowly melting away inside the reactor for months had remained well contained, and nobody in the vicinity of the plant had to be evacuated.

Breeder reactors of this kind are designed to produce plutonium. In theory, they make it possible to generate more energy than they consume, which on paper, makes them sound like some sort of machine for laying philosopher's stones. The reason they have all but disappeared from the industrial landscape is that the proliferation of plutonium is now the subject of international treaties. It is also because the liquid sodium that cools the core has an unfortunate tendency to explode when it comes into contact with water and ignite in contact with air, which poses a number of problems when these reactors are linked up to gigantic steam engines to generate electricity.

When the Enrico Fermi breeder reactor was commissioned in 1963, it was the largest of its kind in the world, and the first to also produce energy on a commercial scale. It represented the same kind of hope for Michigan's industry and local population as the magnox program had across the Atlantic.

IT BEARS REPEATING that, during this period of time, there were cold wars going on, the US was about to become embroiled in the Vietnam War, and all this was happening in the aftermath of two global conflicts that had conditioned psyches across the globe. Every engineer at the forefront of their field had experienced war firsthand. As a result, they knew how important it was, both for the population and the armed forces, to have a stable and powerful source of energy. Walker Cisler was one such engineer. Before becoming the CEO of Detroit Edison, the company that built the Enrico Fermi breeder reactor, he had served as a colonel under Dwight Eisenhower in the Allied Expeditionary Forces. From 1943, he was Chief Engineer, in charge of energy supply and infrastructure. By his own account, he was the man responsible for restoring the electricity supply to Paris after Liberation: thanks to his uniquely American sense of initiative and his skills, which of course were at the cutting edge of engineering, French gas plants had been restored, and were even more efficient than before the war, to France's eternally grateful population.

To say that Walker Cisler was a proponent of nuclear power would be an understatement. Throughout his life, he participated in all kinds of organizations, associations and lobbies in favor of nuclear. To understand his motivations, let us step into his mind for a moment, try to see the world through his eyes, and recall the ravages of night and winter after the electrical infrastructure had buckled under the Nazis' campaign of destruction: starving children, newborn infants frozen to death, tearful old men chilled to the bone, mothers with dark circles under their eyes, hearts turned to leather.

Of course, there was also the scientism and megalomania that shaped Cisler's era and his circle of power, but let us for one moment try to demonstrate the same generosity of spirit this man showed himself. After witnessing the spectacle of humanity in all its wretchedness, returned to its most primitive condition, who would not champion investment in the extraordinary power of the atom at all costs? The chain reaction is a source of heat with infinite power, unparalleled energy density, and, to top it all, its byproduct can be handily recycled into a formidable arsenal of mass deterrence. It would be considered mad, obscurantist or spineless not to try and harness this power.

Walker Cisler was neither mad nor obscurantist, and he certainly wasn't spineless. On the internet today, you can find a photo of him, square-jawed and sporting a confident winner's smile, next to a caption that reads: "King of Oil."

In the background of the black-and-white image, the photography director has placed a cutout of a city with illuminated skyscrapers (the implication being that these are powered by nuclear energy) and, to leave no doubt as to the subject's stature and ambition, his right hand rests confidently on a globe.

This man did everything in his power to ensure that after the war, Detroit Edison, a company that until then had only operated gas power plants, would become a pioneer of commercial nuclear energy. The partial meltdown of his liquid sodium breeder reactor in 1966 did not prevent him from chasing this vision; after all, in the land of free enterprise, what are industrial accidents if not an opportunity to learn and progress?

Two years of shaking hands and playing golf at every good country club in the nation later, Walker Cisler got the green light to build a more conventional nuclear plant: a boiling water reactor to be installed just next to the little breeder model that had gone into meltdown in Frenchtown, Monroe County, on the shores of Lake Erie.

I EXIT THE expressway on the I–75 from Detroit to Toledo, a long, curved diversion delineated by a thick line of white paint and the two-way traffic on the Old Dixie Highway. As I wait for the lights to stop the flow of traffic, I briefly contemplate taking a left towards Sault Ste. Marie on the Ontario border, or a right, due south to Miami. Having arrived a few hours earlier on a transatlantic flight, I am entering the last stage of my errant exploration, the part that could lead me, out of the blue, to the door of a stranger to tell him that I am his daughter. The prospect of instead driving over a thousand miles to go swimming in Biscayne Bay occurs to me, furtively, as a wonderful way of giving up on everything.

But because I'm tired, because I'm hungry and it's late into the night, I continue all the same.

I take a left onto an adjacent route just a few miles down where a round, illuminated sign at least thirty feet tall informs me where I can find the nearest Burger King. Slightly further off the road, a similar sign, rectangular and blue, invites me to stay at America's Best Value Inn and Suites. This is what I decide to do.

It's here, in a room on the first floor, my rental car duly parked in front of the door, that I'm about to spend a night which, unbeknownst to me, will be as short as it is dreadful (though at thirty-two dollars a night, payable upfront, I might have guessed).

Standing between the entrance and the bathroom door, I flick the switch of the single wall lamp fitted with two bulbs, only one of which seems to be working, and see from the dim light that most of the room is taken up by one double and one twin bed. In the absence of a table, chair, or desk, I sit down on the edge of the mattress to tuck into a hot, sweet meat and cheese sandwich, the nearby fast-food restaurant's specialty. The moisture inside has turned the packaging soggy and the whole thing smells of vinegar, gherkins, ink, and wet cardboard. Even though I was starving, two mouthfuls are enough to ruin my appetite altogether.

In the meantime, my eyes have adjusted to the lighting, and I now see strange, pale-gray stains on the carpet and attempt to ascertain how fresh they are. From this moment on, I make every effort not to touch anything, particularly the cold-water faucet in the bathroom, which might possibly be the filthiest object in creation: in the crevice of the plastic handle, where there once must have been a blue dot, there's now a sediment of brownish organic matter, from which thick, black hairs are protruding (and judging from the sinuous texture, they are almost unmistakably pubic hair, though I would have been no less horrified had they been beard clippings).

I turn on the cathode-ray tube television, wondering to myself whether all the equipment in this room predates the fall of the Berlin Wall, and fall asleep with it on to drown out the mournful noises the building's frail plaster walls are incapable of silencing. In a bed that smells of dust, I spend the night battling a nameless anxiety I can only put down to the overpowering influence on my imagination of American cultural production, full of bleak and desolate places like this one. Stamped with the seal of franchised commerce, places like this generally serve as the backdrop for sordid illegal activity: the dark side of the American Dream to which they end up becoming inextricably associated.

Long before daybreak, this irrational anxiety coupled with serious jet lag forces me out early to go on the search for breakfast.

I haven't driven half a mile before I'm parking up again in another strip mall just off the Old Dixie Highway. I leave the car in the empty parking lot of a vast hangar decorated to resemble a ranch from a postcard, where concealed speakers are playing Christmas carols full of bells and good cheer into the night. Cracker Barrel Old Country Store, a chain restaurant slotted in between gift shops (i.e. places filled with objects of no particular use, manufactured in China), opens at five in the morning, just in time, to offer traditional Southern cuisine, no matter where on the New Continent you happen to find yourself.

As I chew pensively on a piece of bacon marinated in maple syrup, the star of the show in a protein-heavy breakfast I wash down with surprisingly good drip coffee served from a

32-ounce jug, dawn begins to break to the sound of "Jingle Bells" as the mist rises from the nearby lake. Sitting in front of a large, prefabricated mantel made of imitation cut stone, I ponder at length the fake Civil War relics, rifles, wooden snowshoes, and photos of Black American families in their Sunday best, all adorned for the season in glittering, festive decorations. I wonder what they could possibly mean, hung here on this fake chimney in the middle of Michigan.

Let me put it bluntly: I hate the United States of America. My gut more so than my brain is responsible for this vague, arbitrary sentiment, which encompasses, indiscriminately and without the slightest pretension to objectivity, an entire half-continent and the whole panoply of what it represents.

I'll spend every minute of my short stay on the outskirts of Detroit measuring the gulf between appearances and reality in this country, since everything I see is perfectly familiar to me. Such is the power of the cliché of America in the world's collective imagination. But every physical interaction with this world feels fake. Every object proves to be hollow, every substance synthetic, every meal consists in some form or other of edible but indistinct matter, recomposed through obscure industrial processes and injected with salt, glucose syrup, and fat. Even the people, shop assistants, servers, drivers, seem to be more concerned with conforming to the caricature of their function rather than simply existing.

This sense of fraud and fakery I attribute partly to the success of the country's audiovisual industry, which has managed to drip feed consumerist illusions down to the very fringes of society, the places economic liberalism has failed to reach with wealth. Since images circulate faster than money, and appearances are easier to conjure up than prosperity, everyone here strives to preserve the former as if it had the power to make up for the absence of the latter, as if it were enough to appear beautiful, kind, or rich as a sort of consolation for never truly being able to be those things.

In between meals primarily composed of corn syrup, I'll be spending the best part of my days in southeastern Michigan behind the wheel of a cheap, plastic, rental car, cruising along the kind of residential streets I have seen time and again on TV: a procession of houses surrounded by lawns and clad in blue-gray wood shingle, each of which is slightly raised off the ground and features a porch. It's hard to imagine anyone walking up these porch steps without a homemade apple pie or a basket of blueberry muffins in hand, tapping on a net-curtained window before the excessively cordial face of a WASP housewife with perfectly styled hair appears like a cog in the machinery.

But how many people know that these days, the wood shingle is most often made of plastic? Just like the little children's playhouses made in China, an eyesore across gardens in just about every residential area of every country across the globe, the villas in this wretched corner of the world are clad with hollow, thermo-molded, mass-colored parts designed to imitate the shape and grain of wood. How many people know that, outside of big, iconic cities, the United States of America largely consists of hundreds of thousands of hectares of these little plastic two-story houses bought on credit, lining the tarmac of residential zones swarming with cars, which are also made of plastic, also bought on credit?

Due to the fact that this reality has been named "economic growth" for over half a century, no one has considered it worth worrying about. Yet any human brain can detect, however vaguely, this discrepancy, this disharmony between what the eyes see and what the body feels. Walking through these streets, even locals can sense deep down that something is not quite right. Matter speaks to our brains via the senses, and here, it's silently crying out that it isn't what it claims to be. This is not a quiet suburb in the land of the free, but a soulless hinterland made out of dead materials, a land impoverished by the excesses of unrepentant capitalism. This silent dissonance gives rise to an unspeakable form of discomfort, and it isn't unreasonable to consider that, in the most fragile minds, this might become a breeding ground for bitter anguish.

DURING THE THIRTY-YEAR golden era of the post-war boom, it was a foregone conclusion, at least in this part of the world, that surrendering civil nuclear power to the laws of the market would create the conditions for collective enrichment that would benefit all.

All over America in the 1960s, consortia of private investors had formed to buy nuclear reactors and all their paraphernalia from leading industrialists, whose profits, of course, were to trickle down in the form of employment. Meanwhile, the huge quantities of cheap electricity generated by these new power plants would not only bring comfort to households, but also increase the efficiency of factories, whose profits, in turn, would trickle down, and so on and so forth. The sum of individual interests, needless to say, was in the general interest of the public as a whole.

Nuclear power plants were springing up all over the country and with the miracle of the free market in full swing, no two nuclear power plants in the country looked the same.

Every call for tender was issued by groups with different priorities, whims and budgets, which meant that industrial bidders, under maximum competitive pressure, all found themselves in a race for a share in the market.

And so it came to be that technologies of all shapes, sizes and combinations, made by a whole host of different manufacturers, were being tested out all over the US.

There's a common adage in the nuclear industry that goes as follows: "In France, there's a different type of cheese for each day of the year but only one type of nuclear power plant. In the USA, the opposite is true."

In 1968, Detroit Edison opted to buy a boiling water reactor from General Electric, a machine that differs from pressurized water models in that it only has one cooling loop. The liquid that keeps the chain reaction under control by cooling the reactor is the same liquid that turns to steam and drives the turbines and generators. These generators, incidentally, were ordered from another company, English Electric, which would ship monumental 1,200-megawatt machines from its factories in central England. Each blade on their titanic rotors measured at least the size of a fully grown adult.

This curious translatlantic pairing was formed because these were the two bidders proposing the best performance and price, the latter, it has to be said, being the decisive factor. The greatest swindle of liberalism consists in making people believe that competition enables companies to buy the "best technology at the best price," when in reality, the technology being purchased is "the best we can hope for," because the seller has had to cut corners to keep costs at a minimum.

So Detroit Edison bought a nuclear power plant at *the best price*, in the form of a mismatched kit, and proceeded to take two decades to get it to a point where it was more or less operational. Because all the promises made by these different vendors culminated in shortcomings, particularly in matters of safety: shortcomings that led to incessant budget overruns, until the company was left with no money and not even a half-functional nuclear plant. A new consortium of investors then had to be created to generate funds, which in turn led to a sustained increase in the price of electricity for customers who, having no obligation or desire to pay more, turned en masse to other electricity suppliers. Needless to say, these are not the ideal conditions for successfully assembling a nuclear power plant.

You arrive on the scene in the midst of this industrial debacle in 1978.

In South Korea, the child with the round eyes is getting bigger every day. Her mother has already begun a new job but hasn't yet fallen in love with another man. Meanwhile, you settle down in a suburb of southern Michigan with your legitimate family, which now comprises two little girls aged six and four, both born in Taiwan, and their mother, who must either be very forgiving with regard to you, or realistic with regard to her own situation, given that she is about to give birth to your third child (another will be born later, in 1980).

The English Electric turbines and generators, which were purchased ten years prior and shipped in parts from Rugby, England, had just been assembled in a hangar the length of a stadium, and given your expertise in the field, you'd been asked to supervise the commissioning process. Little did you know that it would be another ten years before the electricity generated by these obsolete machines would finally light up Detroit.

It wouldn't be long before the Three Mile Island accident would leave your industry hanging in the balance. But the Fermi 2 construction site didn't need to wait for this stroke of bad luck. For years it had already been mired by the paradoxical injunctions of the free market.

What were you doing getting yourself bogged down in the midst of all this? On the desolate outskirts of the most dangerous city in the US, on the shores of the world's most polluted lake, embroiled in the construction of a bankrupt nuclear power plant that was obsolete before it was even commissioned, in the imminent shockwave of the biggest nuclear accident in history, you were preparing to spend the rest of your life living the American dream in little suburban area with nothing going for it, duty-bound to support a wife who kept falling pregnant. Whether you loved her, or had fallen back in love with her, or loved her some of the time, whatever feelings you were caught up in, you made some serious compromises with yourself.

It's a 1977 Cadillac Coupe DeVille, brown or rust, a model that had quarter windows with a cream vinyl frame, a reinterpretation of the opera window to suit the tastes of the time.

Every morning of the week, you reverse down the short, wide driveway in front of the double garage of your detached house and drive slowly through the residential cul-de-sac lined with manicured lawns, flowerbeds and saplings, switching on the car radio just before turning left onto Highway 233.

How remarkably banal, those agricultural landscapes divided into squares by secondary roads, homogeneous monocultures interspersed with small residential neighborhoods, wide driveways unfurling on either side of the main road in loops to make it easier for big cars to turn around, each with the same lawn, flowerbeds, and ornamental trees.

You have an hour's drive through Michigan ahead of you, always in heavy traffic, as every human being over the age of sixteen here travels alone in their own car. The car radio intermittently informs you of Jimmy Carter's tribulations in between disco hits (Donna Summer, Chic, Gloria Gaynor, music you don't like but find yourself humming to sometimes, your brain absorbing everything like a sponge). There's no two ways about it, that socialist president is in the process of disgracing the West and killing off the nuclear industry, all the while flattering himself that he is working in the interests of world peace. Hypocrisy and kowtowing, clear as day.

It doesn't take two months for the security staff to start letting you in without asking to see your pass. You always choose the same spot in the parking lot and back the car in (which takes some maneuvering without power steering), as you prefer to do so in the morning rather than at the end of a long day. Engine off, you grab the briefcase from under the passenger seat, stretch your legs out the open door, then slam it loudly shut.

Once you hear the familiar click of the key turning in the lock, you walk around to the other side of the car and mechanically test the second door to make sure it's locked, because central locking hasn't yet been invented. This is a useless procedure, because you're the only one to ever get in or out of the vehicle, always via the same door. The wife has her own car, of course, a family model for taking the kids to and from football games and piano lessons in between supermarket runs. But habits that cost nothing are the hardest to break.

You're forty-three years old the first time you park your car in the vast parking lot on the Enrico Fermi electro-nuclear site, and until you reach fifty-three, the only thing that changes periodically in this American routine, five days a week, fifty weeks a year, is the make of car you drive.

Through delays and prorogations, from adjournment to moratorium, from postponement to indefinite deferral, over the course of a decade, as the boiling water reactor construction site sinks into a humiliating state of semi-bankruptcy, you get in and out of your Cadillac DeVille, your Ford Thunderbird, your Pontiac Firebird, your Chevrolet Corvette, holding a briefcase full of annotated reports, revised documents, amended reverse schedules. Without so much as a backwards glance at the little dome of the ill-fated breeder reactor to the right of the parking lot that went into meltdown a decade prior, you go through the automatic double door into a narrow, linoleum-covered corridor, nod to the security guard and telephone operator behind the closed reception desk, before making your way down the dark hallway to the office you share with your assistant. There, you put down your briefcase, change into your uniform, put on your helmet, and head to the turbine room to meet your team and give your orders for the day.

By sundown, or nightfall, depending on the season, you're back in your car again, driving across the agricultural plains, listening to the same music, this time interspersed with the evening presenters, speakers with nasal voices you've become accustomed to, just like disco and Jimmy Carter.

Back at home, your little girls jump into your arms (at least while they're still children) subjecting you to a ritual deluge of noise and disorder, which you invariably put an end to by taking a candy out of your pocket for each of them. Then, as the cliché that has become your life as an upper middle class American breadwinner dictates, you put on a pair of slippers and stretch out in "your" armchair with the newspaper, still rolled up in a plastic pouch, that the boy on a bicycle throws onto your front yard each morning.

With its two tall, magnificent cooling chimneys coiffed with thick, white plumes of smoke, Fermi 2 is a picture-perfect nuclear power plant, served up on a generous concrete plateau on a marshy strip of land set in a small inlet.

To reach it requires crossing vast fields that sit beside reed forests populated by wading birds, ducks, and probably swans, before going right to the end of a long, residential lane built upon what appears to have originally been a dyke, on the other side of Swan Creek. From there, you have to trespass onto a small yard with an American flag flying above it, behind a detached house clad with gray, plastic, imitation-wood shingles, to get the best view of the plant, and if you listen carefully, you can hear its chimneys whispering their weariness to a white sky that doesn't care.

Of all the power plants that have marked your life, this is the first to fit the stereotypical image of the nuclear industry.

Despite the fact that most of the world's cooling chimneys belong to coal-fired power plants, and many nuclear power plants don't have them, these great concrete cones have become the main symbol of the commercial nuclear industry in the eyes of the general public.

Yet in all the fifteen years you've worked in the industry, you've never come into contact with one. And for good reason: before you were given this assignment in Monroe, you'd never been this far from the sea.

Nuclear power stations on the coast don't have chimneys. This is because their outflow pipes discharge heated water directly into the sea, which can accommodate water a few degrees warmer than its natural temperature without any issue. In a river or a lake, this would be more harmful to the ecosystem, hence the towers, which serve to release residual heat into the air rather than the water.

You grew up on the shores of the Irish Sea and when you left it was for the English Channel, the Celtic Sea, and the coastal waters where the UK had erected its lighthouses and cast its buoys. You gave up the ships but never the sea, because Wylfa took you back to the coast of Wales, Linkou to the Taiwan Strait, and Kori to the East Sea. Until the two Fermi towers came to obstruct your horizons, you had always lived in the mighty presence of the sea, in the infinite movement and agitation of the plains, in the wind and the clouds, in the cradle of storms, commerce and cultural exchange, the lands of legends and literature.

At the very least, Lake Erie fulfills the essential function assigned to vast bodies of water by romantics, which is to bring even civilization's most sprawling landscapes to a halt by stopping the proliferation of buildings in its tracks. Unconquerable expanses allow minds and eyes to lose themselves for a while in misty voids and uncertain horizons.

But this lake, with its eroding concrete shores turning to rubble and rust, with its ecosystem that is periodically suffocated by algae, dying from the industrialization of its shores… this lake simply cannot be enough to fill the void in your heart that the sea has left behind. Anyone who has loved those ferocious waters and untamed coastlines could never be swept away by something so sad and sedentary.

How long was it before you registered the magnitude of everything you had lost?

Just as in the forest, you can feel the proximity of a stream on your skin, at the coast you know the sea is there before you see or hear it. And I cannot for one moment believe that this visceral emotion does not live inside you like an addiction. Here, for the first time, you've found yourself living far from the salt spray and the breath of the open sea. Your freedom, that familiar presence that never failed to awaken your senses, has been amputated. And here, living with this privation, this ablation, I know: you've given up, surrendered. You've become bitter without the sea.

THE PROBLEM WAS, they were incompetent. Perhaps in other fields, they would have been perfectly capable. In the past they might have made excellent grocery store managers or been exemplary telephone exchange operators. But in the nuclear power industry, they were utterly lousy, and it was for precisely this reason, a "lack of competence in the operational management of a nuclear power plant at all levels of management," that the US Nuclear Regulatory Commission (NRC) repeatedly blocked the commissioning of the Fermi 2 reactor.

In 1985, Detroit Edison had just obtained authorization (not without difficulty) to begin low-power testing, after four long years spent overhauling the plant's circuits and revising its safety procedures from top to bottom at the express request of the NRC. Aside from the gross engineering errors and basic operating problems identified, which, as we will later see, would continue to wreak havoc, the control room (essentially the brain of the plant) had been so poorly designed with such a catastrophically illegible dashboard, that it took the nuclear authority's inspectors thirty-three A4 pages of small print to list the minimum corrective measures to be taken before the machine could be started up. This included, most notably, finding the missing binders containing the instruction manual for the reactor.

Once authorization was obtained, everything seemed to be on track for the first power-up, only when the time finally came to get down to business, just a few hours from the crucial moment, an operator inadvertently hit the control rod command button and accidentally set off a chain reaction.

The whole thing sounds like a scene lifted straight from an episode of *The Simpsons*. The nuclear inspectors make a surprise visit to the nuclear plant, Homer falls asleep on the big red button, all the alarms go off without waking him up, and in the end, his dog saves the day by pulling the emergency switch. Instead this scene comes from an NRC report, a transcription consisting solely of real-life events; even these are embellished in a certain way, the more tragic aspects obfuscated by a mixture of simple formulations and mysterious abbreviations. This is the kind of report that makes humanity despair.

Two weeks later, during a second test run, the reactor's water supply pump was damaged due to mishandling.

That same week, the emergency cooling system was discovered to be malfunctioning due to a design error as opposed to a breakdown. The very same design error was then found in the emergency diesel generators (surprise!), which, it was subsequently discovered, had never been working in the first place.

To top it all, someone finally realized that a valve in the containment vessel, the one used to retain radioactive products, had been left open for two months without anyone noticing.

Given the scale of the existing and potential problems, the NRC finally decided at the end of 1985, after six months of calamitous tests, to suspend Fermi 2 operations until all corrective measure had been taken, starting with the replacement of the entire management team by personnel trained to work in a nuclear power plant.

Four months later, 3,000 miles away, an RBMK reactor exploded. It was Chernobyl. The investigation would show, albeit much later, that the accident was the consequence of individual and collective errors, a tragic chain of unpreparedness and ignorance that, unfortunately, was neither fundamentally unique to RBMK reactors nor the Soviet Union.

As the first major and deadly nuclear accident, Chernobyl prompted all countries with nuclear power plants to question the safety of their own facilities. It was only then that the good people of the United States realized, to their incredulity, that they had a hundred or so nuclear power plants on their territory, and that it was absolutely impossible to measure the risk inherent in their design. And for good reason: the free market had been so successful that no two power plants in the country were the same.

At a parliamentary hearing in the wake of the Soviet disaster in May 1986, NRC representatives presented the astonished representatives of the people with a list of sixteen nuclear power plants they deemed to be of concern due to known manufacturing defects or the patent incompetence of their personnel. The most astonishing thing was not that Fermi 2 was on the list, but that fifteen others were also included for equally or even more staggering irregularities. Thirty years on, most of these plants are still in operation.

It would have undoubtedly been wise for you to start looking for a new job straight after the first tests, the first obvious failures, the first humiliations. Working for an external contractor, you could have asked for a transfer, a new assignment. But years had gone by, you'd put down roots for the children, and without realizing it, you'd begun the cruel descent into unemployability. After the age of forty, middle and senior managers become expensive, start to lose touch with the times, and are too far into their own fields of specialization. And you, having made turbines and generators for nuclear power plants your area of expertise, now found yourself stuck in the mud just like the industry to which you had sold the best years of your life. After Three Mile Island, Chernobyl was the final straw. The market for nuclear power was once again at a standstill, and those who had a job in the field clung to it, especially given the generally high salary.

At every fork in the road, you made the most reasonable choice given your responsibilities. You had watched on as your children were born, one after the other, without ever asking yourself whether you were happy. Officially, you had four by this point: three girls and a boy. Over time, you forgot about the other woman and the other child; all you knew is that they were no longer in Korea. Opportunities to buy, sell and build houses came one after another, each at the initiative of your wife, who went from kitchen-to-kitchen with varying degrees of contentment, always with that mix of authority and servitude common among women who don't work, while your own career dragged on, bringing increasing dissatisfaction and anxiety.

At the same time, your salary was rising ahead of inflation, you continued to buy yourself ever more expensive cars and motorcycles, and though there were times when you felt old and trapped, you weren't in the habit of thinking about it too much.

Money doesn't buy happiness, but it does provide possibilities for escape. By investing in hobbies for rich people and buying increasingly bigger houses, at least you had an extensive domestic space to dilute your regrets in. By now, you were spending most of your time cooped up in the workshop in your garage.

Age was the one sphere in which you continued to move forward; going gray, gaining weight, never tiring of tinkering in your workshop, cleaning, unscrewing, polishing, repairing, changing parts, preventing breakdowns. In the privacy of your garage, where time was suspended and belonged to you alone, you regained the decision-making power and entrepreneurial freedom that your job no longer offered. Each of the mechanical collectibles you now owned required specific care, each engine had its own unique combustion secrets, sounds, complications, whims and smells that made it resemble a living thing.

In the workshop, you installed an intercom, and when your wife called you for dinner, you crossed the small section of the yard separating you from the house via a ribbon of beige gravel, and entered the kitchen via the French door, your clothes laden with the smell of solvents that would forever waft through the childhood memories of your four kids. It only took you a few minutes to polish off your meal, barely interacting with your nearest and dearest, before you'd head straight back to your garage and remain there until nightfall. In the solitary company of those engines, you gained a sense of purpose you couldn't seem to find anywhere else.

The mastery of each sequence, from mental visualization to diagnosis of the problem, from ordering parts to patiently assembling, disassembling and reassembling them, the ineffable satisfaction of hearing the explosive roar of the machine, the feeling of having effectively transformed the world, of having drawn matter out of its inertia to infuse it with movement, force and drive, and of having done so alone, using only your brain and hands. This was the only pleasure your existence still gave you, but it was a great one. You were, of course, an inadequate father. What would I have made of a generous man, close to his children, generously providing for his family, beaming as he shared the things he loved, organizing weekends of laughter and adventure for his merry band of offspring in the spectacular natural settings of Michigan? Mediocrity, withdrawal, and gloom are easier for me to imagine because they help keep you at a safe distance.

WHEN YOU BUY "the best technology at the best price," and insist on employing slackers to run a nuclear power plant, this is what you end up with: in 1988, twenty years after construction began, Detroit Edison was finally granted authorization to produce electricity at its boiling water power plant. Problems with vibrations coming from the enormous English turbine were well-known and documented, but everyone acted as though these design flaws would disappear of their own accord, perhaps thanks to divine intervention.

Barely six months after the plant was first launched, the main turbine was vibrating so much that the emergency stop system was triggered to do precisely what it is designed to do: preventively shut down the reactor. After a quick analysis, the incident was attributed to the lubricant cooling system, which had been tinkered with just before the huge machine was recommissioned.

Nine months later, the same vibrations triggered another emergency shutdown. This time, it was decided that the best thing to do would be to deactivate the emergency shutdown circuit (i.e. silence the messenger) until the next scheduled refueling.

It therefore took another six months before the cover was finally opened so that the turbine could be examined. It was then discovered that several of the blades on the three low-pressure turbines had been seriously damaged, and others completely broken, which in retrospect explained the high levels of vibration that the safety system failed to detect since it had been switched off.

The problem was that there were no spare parts in stock (perhaps this hadn't been included in the purchase price). A decision was made to carry out a major repair operation, staggered in stages over several years. Firstly, all the broken blades were to be removed until the supplier was able to produce replacements. Those that were the most worn but still more or less intact were to be replaced with whatever spare parts were in stock and then sent back to the factory for repair. The remainder were to be kept where they were, despite being in a bad state of disrepair, in the hope that by the next scheduled shutdown, the worn blades would come back refurbished to be used as replacements. This process would be repeated at each scheduled reactor shutdown for fuel change.

Perhaps it's worth pointing out here that shutting down a reactor, and therefore halting electricity production, is extremely costly. This is why short-sighted accounting logic dictates that all repairs should coincide with planned reactor shutdowns, even though it would be common sense on a machine of this size that poses this great a hazard to carry out such repairs as a matter of urgency.

But, after all, Detroit Edison was a heavily indebted company. This nuclear power plant had been guzzling billions of dollars for twenty years and had only just begun operations. Hence, the program for this vast, staggered DIY job was hastily validated for lack of an economic alternative, and the reactor vessels were sealed before all the pieces of broken blades were found because, what with all the vibrations, God only knows where they had gone.

Three months later, there was yet another emergency shutdown, this time due to abnormal movements in the thrust bearing (the part that holds the turbine shaft in place). Entire rows of blades were missing, and the wretched beast, already plagued by vibrations, was now more unstable than ever. But the pragmatism of nuclear power plant managers knows no bounds: it would suffice to turn off the automatic shutdown circuit linked to the thrust bearing. After all, what's the point in being constantly alerted to a problem you've already decided to deal with later?

A year went by with heads in the sand before the reactor crashed again due to the vibrations: the blades removed from the low-pressure turbines had left the next row of blades exposed to quantities of steam they had not been designed to withstand. As a result, some of the blades had broken off, and now had to be removed as well.

Six months down the line, the parts finally arrived to replace the first blades to have been removed, though not the most recently damaged ones. Knowing these parts were very fragile, a decision was made to keep them in place (touch wood) until the next scheduled refueling—two years later.

Of course, it was less than a year before the emergency shutdown circuits tripped the reactor again. This time, for a change, the incident had nothing to do with the turbines, but it's worth reporting because it's funny all the same. One day in August 1993, an operator had the bright idea of pulling off a piece of tape (!) from one of the levers in the control room, thus inadvertently triggering an alarm indicating that the water level in the reactor was too high. In the panic that ensued, the operators pushed buttons they shouldn't have, throwing the cooling system out of whack, setting off just over a hundred light bulbs on the control room dashboard at the same time. What followed was a farcical scene: the operators, who didn't know what they were doing as it was, could no longer see what was going on at all because half of the lights in the control room had blown. No one could tell anymore whether the various valves were open or closed, whether water and steam were gushing out where they weren't supposed to be, whether the emergency circuits were still active or not. Cue close-up of sweating faces, etc. A valuable lesson was learned from this momentous day of panic: in the future, it might be worth thinking twice before fiddling with a piece of tape in the control room.

Finally, the inevitable happened, on Christmas Day of all days.

On December 25, 1993, the power plant began to shake all over, and the tremors could be felt all the way to the control room. For two very long minutes, extremely loud and completely abnormal noises emanated from the turbine room, followed by several explosions. All of the nuclear power plant's alarms, or at least all those that hadn't previously been silenced, began to sound and flash at the same time: seismic alarms, fire alarms, panic stations.

The operators on duty that day, by this point either drunk or at least heavily bloated and nursing a seasonal hangover, were not the most confident bunch and did not know what procedure to follow (had they ever been told?). Some of them nevertheless took the initiative to don protective clothing and made their way tearful and trembling towards the noise in an attempt to identify the nature of the problem(s). What they discovered when they opened the door to the turbine hall was something that can only have looked like the end of days: infernal heat, billowing smoke and the most almighty din; deafening banging and hissing sounds escaping from the eviscerated metallic reactor vessel, in a shower of steam, completely engulfed in flames. The engine room was both flooded and on fire.

Thirty-seven minutes later—an eternity—the fire department assigned to the Fermi site arrived on the scene. Of course, these young men were just as ill-prepared; each of their simulation exercises had been as slapdash as the next, and no one really knew how the protective wear was supposed to be worn. The gear included, among other gadgets, a motion detector whose function is to signal a man down. Except these detectors hadn't been serviced and were not set up properly, which meant that they kept going off for no reason at all, and like the ludicrous cherry on this rather tragic cake, continued to emit a screeching sound to add to the chaos. Encumbered by their own gear, clumsy, distraught and literally tripping over themselves, the cavalry proved to be of little help.

The subsequent investigation determined that one of the blades, which had been showing signs of wear for years and whose replacement had been postponed several times, had finally failed while the machine was running at full speed. When it finally broke off, it tore through the turbine casing and all the surrounding machinery, including part of the adjacent heat exchanger, a hydrogen supply pipe (hydrogen being a gas that ignites upon contact with air) and a lubricating oil supply pipe, setting the entire assembly on fire. At the same time, the ruptured heat exchanger had released immense quantities of very high-temperature steam (which, we might recall, comes directly from the reactor in a boiling-water power plant), along with some six hundred and fifty hectoliters of oil and twenty thousand hectoliters of water fresh from Lake Erie.

This merry mixture of hot, flammable and radioactive fluids had completely drowned the turbine hall and spilled over into the rest of the power plant, right down to the storage room for spent fuel (also highly radioactive), which proceeded to bathe under six feet of this toxic broth for several weeks.

Luckily, nobody died in this disaster. But it took over two years to clean up the damage and get the plant up and running again.

I won't go into all the subsequent problems here, since, of course, this disastrous event did not even mark a turning point in the plant's history. Once it was recommissioned, the Fermi 2 reactor suffered one chronic illness after the next: vibrations coming from the big English turbine, managerial negligence, penny-pinching, and incompetent operations staff.

Where were you, what were you doing as, month after month, year after year, the difficulties, problems and accidents caused by your big English turbine continued to pile up? Just like the degenerative and incurable illness of an elderly patient keeps the family doctor in a job, the vibrations of your turbine kept you occupied to the end of your career. You wrote reports that would never be read, wrote letters that went unanswered, sent out fruitless warnings about the potential dangers of postponing various repairs and part changes, and attended meetings where your cautioning went unheeded. And then, you went home each night, wondering whether the damaged blades, the busted bearings, and unstable shafts would one day end up killing someone.

At the same time, you cashed in your monthly salary, locked yourself away in your workshop, bought vintage cars and motorcycles and sank into a silence that grew heavier with each day.

On Judgment Day, you will not only be charged with the things you've done, but also the things you haven't done.

AFTER THE DOORBELL rings, the rest of the scene is more or less a foregone conclusion. The door opens and, following a moment of embarrassed astonishment, the old man's face begins to tremble, there's a tear in his eye, he breaks down with emotion. The next shot shows a close-up of his hands clasping hers, and the credits roll to music that is both poignant and hopeful.

In a more dramatic version, this would be the moment the character is revealed to be a real bastard: distraught, panic-stricken, gesticulating in surprise, the old man delivers a stream of invective, thus validating one of the narrator's initial hypotheses.

In either version, on screen or on the page, the purpose of the scene is to be final, conclusive, cathartic.

Reality, much to our chagrin, is never that simple.

In reality, there is nothing conclusive about the moment a

woman rings a man's doorbell to tell him she is his daughter. Quite the reverse: it is precisely that moment when everything gets muddled up and trouble begins.

I once spoke about this project to a relatively elderly man, a man I sensed had every reason to believe he could end up with a situation like this on his hands. He remarked that the late reappearance of an illegitimate child would ultimately pose questions of a financial and legal rather than emotional nature. This, of course, had never occurred to me.

To be clear, not only are such questions of no interest to me, they positively repulse me. The idea that this man and his entourage, this group of strangers who, for all intents and purposes, are my half brothers and sisters, might suspect me of trying to lay claim to their money is one that absolutely disgusts me.

The stretch of this road that runs through Michigan is called the Riga Highway, but once it crosses the border to Ohio, it becomes Washburn Road. On either side of this perfectly straight strip of tarmac, the vast, manicured lands allotted for extensive agriculture occasionally give way to residential zones that might have been grand had they not been drowning in these enormous rural flatlands.

I arrive at my destination at the point in the road where a dozen monumental villas are vying with one another to be the most kitsch. Each has been built according to its owners' whims on plots of land eight acres apiece. The vastness of each plot of land has evidently done nothing to encourage modesty; certain villas feature Roman pillars, others medieval turrets, and each plot has several driveways with a small rotary in front of the main entrance, pathways sprayed with Roundup and artificial ponds that most likely smell of chlorine.

I already knew this thanks to Google Maps' street view tool, but nothing beats being here in the flesh to experience the true ugliness of it all. His house looks like an English cottage in the way the Disney castle resembles Neuschwanstein, with all due respect to differences in scale. The shapes, the colors, and the large, dark, sloping roofs are all nods to the houses that inspired them, only these roofs are not thatched but tiled with synthetic materials. All the volumes are hypertrophied, the white facades punctured with haughty PVC bow windows in lieu of wooden frames. The property has no fewer than nine garage doors, four on one wing of the house, and five others attached to an annex at the end of the garden that mimics the shapes of a small manor.

On either side of Washburn Road, a ditch separates the road from other properties, and suffice to say that nothing, absolutely nothing at all, has been designed to enable a car to park there. Unless you're a local, there are only two possibilities here: either someone is expecting you, in which case, you approach that person's property via their driveway, or you carry on driving straight for the next twelve miles.
In a fictional script, this would never have happened. With all the naivety of a bourgeois-bohemian who is only familiar with the large cities of Europe, the scriptwriter's line of thought would have been as follows: at this point in the story, the narrator is still hesitant (will she or won't she ring?) so she goes to park her car in the neighborhood and waits discreetly, engine and headlights off, to see if anyone appears at the window or comes out of the house, for example, to pick up the mail from the mailbox. No screenwriter would consider the possibility that there are inhabited places on

earth in front of which it's simply impossible to leave a car parked, let alone discreetly.

Nothing could be more out of the ordinary, more sensational or remarkable than the appearance of my gray plastic rental car this morning, parked in the middle of the American road network where such an eventuality is simply unthinkable. Every passing car slows down to see if anyone is inside the suspicious vehicle, each of them probably expecting to find a bearded man with a turban or some other kind of terrorist. The thoughtful postman goes so far as to stop and roll down his window, forcing me to do the same, to assure him that no, thank you, everything is fine, no, my car hasn't broken down, and no, really, I don't need any help.

At this point I'm certain that someone will eventually report my presence to one of those private security companies whose job it is to ensure a quiet life for the inhabitants of residential areas like this, so I decide to move out of the area and park at the edge of a field before returning on foot to prowl the perimeter of the villa in question. But because of the strictly car-centric conception of America's urban sprawl, there is nothing discreet about being a pedestrian here. I blend into the landscape like a cow on an ice floe. In this country where nobody ever walks, in a neighborhood where only residents stop, I'm now wandering in the rain, a hooded silhouette, my only obvious purpose being to take photos of a house that clearly isn't mine.

If the police were to ask me, at this precise moment, what I'm doing here, I wouldn't know how to respond. I'd end up at the police station and I'd probably even be banned from visiting the US. What a quixotic ending that would be.

I had never imagined that the choice would end up being mine. A mixture of naivety and magical thinking led me to believe that headwinds or fate would intervene somewhere along the way and absolve me of this decision. Even more likely, I thought that death would put an end to my investigation. I imagined my genitor, taken from the lives of his loved ones and no longer the subject of my inquiry, forever to remain a specter, the sum of hypotheses and probabilities, a fictional character.

A Christmas wreath hangs on the imposing wrought iron electric gate ('tis the season). But in my current frame of mind, I take it for a funeral wreath.

So what now? Am I supposed to ring the bell? Trade in the familiarity of the questions I have carried with me all my life for the mediocrity of reality? Forever erase the distant, dreamlike images that have been my bedrock and replace them with the mundane substance of a real-life person who will inevitably turn out to be a disappointment?

What kind of book could I possibly write beneath the burden of such a sad reality?

I HAVE TURNED up in your life at the point when nothing else can happen to you.

Inside the brick walls of the big house of your dreams, silence falls like dust on the vast collection of your inanimate possessions, the remnants of a lifetime's accumulation.

I imagine you there, in your living space reduced to one single bedroom with an en-suite bathroom, perhaps moving around with the aid of a walker. There's a TV constantly on in the background but you can't see the images because your sight has gone and you can't understand the words because the world has changed.

You've been too old for too long now. Everything has closed up inside you. In the shrunken sphere of your old age, all there is room for is routine, the things you know and recognize, the carefully tiled ground of certainty where nothing can grow now. Ground that is shrinking. The domain of ideas, the field of ambitions, everything that once was your life is now nothing but an enclosure where resentment clings like poison ivy to the dead stump of your hopes. There's no space in this sad panorama for the child you left behind forty years ago.

A few months ago, I wrote to you and you didn't reply. You held my letter in your hands, the one in which I introduced myself under a name that is no longer mine, a name that likely brought to mind a woman in tears and a little girl with fine black curls. A long time ago, you made the trip from the United States to South Korea to see them again, leaving behind your books and promises. That was the last time you held them in your arms, in what must now seem like someone else's life.

But who is the person in the letter, taking the name of a ghost to introduce herself? You don't know. You don't know what kind of woman she has become and you have no desire to find out. In the tiny, fossilized garden of your existence, no question can take root, no curiosity can flourish. At your age, any strength you have left you need to save for dying. I'm here behind the wall, on the other side of your net-curtained windows, standing in the rain beneath the same sky as you, an unlikely visitor taking white cold breaths in front of the low automatic gate that already has your funeral wreath hanging from it.

All you would have to do is stand up, open the curtains, and there, under a black parka with a waterproof hood, behind the rain-spattered glasses of a stranger who looks just like you, you would find the remnants of a love story you've long since forgotten. Under the gray December sky, outside your house, beyond the brash decor of your old age, I'm a shadow come from afar, the memory of an embrace, the vestiges of an emotion, the living product of a feeling from the past, the stifled regrets, the buried remorse, a revenant standing at your window.

I won't ring your doorbell. It took for me to come all the way here, to cross the ocean, to feel the possibility of this encounter at the tips of my fingers, to be able to say that nothing was stopping me, neither geographical constraints nor twists of fate, in order to finally choose, not to step back, not to retreat, but to turn my back on you.

What remains in you, bitter old man, of your hopes and desires and all the things you once loved?

As I turn away, never to meet you again, I see it written on the low wall of your gate, engraved in capital letters on a slate plaque: the name you've chosen for your house. The incurable nostalgia that inhabits you is all there in this name, which reads in Welsh like a sigh. *Sŵn y môr.*

As a child you would listen to it in the summer, lying on the warm stone of the breakwater. It tasted of sea spray and the power of eternity.

And as you lie there with your eyes closed, can you still hear it now? *Sŵn y môr:* the song of the sea.

© Sophie Bassouls

RINNY GREMAUD

Born in 1977 in Busan, South Korea, Rinny Gremaud is a journalist and novelist. She is the editor-in-chief of *T* magazine *(Le Temps)* and lives in Lausanne. Her first book, *Un monde en toc, (All the World's a Mall)* was published in 2018. *Generator* is her first novel.

HOLLY JAMES

Holly James is a translator (MA in Literary Translation, University of Portsmouth, UK) of French, German and Spanish, living and teaching in England. She has translated professionally for over five years now and has worked with Sabine Wespieser Editions *(The Favourite* by Jollien Fardel, 2023) and with Semiotext(e)/Serpent's Tail on two novels by Constance Debré, most recently *Love Me Tender* in 2022.